Chronicles of Hart:
Island

Katlin Murray

For Al.

ACKNOWLEDGMENTS

As always I would like to thank my family for their incredible support, my husband Al for the amazing cover art, my father and father-in –law for their willingness to read, and help with edits. I am truly grateful for you all.

FAREWELL

When Grace awoke, it was to the sound of hammering, yet again. The air was still with an awkward silence, thick with anticipation and stagnant from the smells of repair.

She pulled back the covers, welcoming the cool morning air. Dressing slowly, she padded across the room to unbolt her door as quietly as possible. She slipped on her running shoes before stepping through into the hall, nearly forgetting for the third morning in a row. The welt on her foot where she had stepped on a loose nail reminded her to be careful. She walked through the hall, wary of loose nails and shards of splintered wood as she paced down the stairs onto the main level, eager for breakfast.

She made her way through the debris and plastic coverings into the kitchen hoping to brew a pot of coffee before her visitors had to hit the road. She had no such luck. The kitchen was void of electrical power and cabinets. Standing by the counter she flicked at the light switch repeatedly until she remembered why the lights were not responding. She had forgotten in her lethargic state that her kitchen had become a construction zone, again.

The refrigerator was beginning to smell of mold. She opened it and closed it again with a frown, the putrid smell wafted towards her and reminded her of the cooler they were now keeping their cold food in.

The wild storm had certainly taken a toll on the house. Water had bled from every wall, pooling towards the main floor in a waterfall off of the main stairway. The most damage had come from the water that had found its way through the floor and into the walls on the main floor. Now they crumbled at her touch. The plaster had deteriorated to dust, clinging on out of familiarity, a light breeze could collapse the whole interior. Grace shuddered at the thought.

The restoration company had insisted that they move to a hotel, for their safety, while the house was renovated. Grace had refused, much to their dismay. She knew she wouldn't be safer anywhere else.

The normally quiet house was bustling with life. Construction crews had been working since seven, a steady pattering of hammers and shouting echoed throughout the property. Grace listened eagerly to the chatter of workers. Finally she heard the clattering of Agent King. His loud footfalls racing across the damaged, protesting floorboards overhead as he packed his bag in haste, wary of the scolding he was about to receive from his partner for sleeping past his alarm again.

Now that the rest of the house was awake, their guests were packing up to head home.

Agents King and Chung had wrapped up their vacation in Monticello. They had managed a full two days of down time, much of which was utilized by King to re-train and hire new security and help Ethan deal with insurance companies. The bustling atmosphere around the house left Grace feeling outside herself, as though she were watching her own life from the sidelines, played back to her in fast forward, the days had sped by.

The two were required to head back to the Washington field office to file reports on the escapades of the previous week. Chung seemed eager to get back before King found himself another case to chase.

The two grudgingly made their way to the boarded up front foyer of the Evans' estate, hastily trying to leave without causing a scene in front of the on-looking construction crew that had grown suspiciously silent in anticipation of a long goodbye.

Chung leaned in to Jenny with a loathing glance at the worker across the hall.

"Jen you promise you'll stay for a bit, just until I can get the security up at your place?" Chung looked to his sister with sincere eyes, keeping his voice low.

After all she had been through in the last couple of weeks, Chung felt that she would be better off somewhere where she could talk about it. If she went home she would be alone, with no one to talk to about the weeks she had just spent behind the veil of the FBI. Jenny wasn't coping well with the information she had gathered during the amusement park escapades Ethan had taken them on. She was too far in to back out now, and going home would mean closing the door on all that she had just discovered about the Hart cases. He didn't think she was ready for that just yet. Grace and Ethan could help her adjust to the knowledge of his latest case within the safety of a well secured home. He couldn't ask for more. As he waited with bated breath for her to defy him, as she was prone to do, he watched her face contorting in contemplation.

She was at least thinking it over, he could still hope. Finally she replied slowly.

"I promise... but call me, okay?" She pointed to his phone, "Do the safety dance when you get in."

It was an old family joke, reminding him to call when he was home safe. After last week, she was more worried about him than ever. The realization that his position at the Federal Bureau was not a desk job had set her nerves on fire, she went cold at the thought of her brother racing through life with a gun at his back. Any wrong move and he could be gone before she could count a heartbeat. She bit her tongue again as the inevitable passed through her mind.

Chung wasn't even the least bit surprised that she had begun to name terms. Jenny wasn't one to just say yes to him, even if it was for her own good.

"You're starting to sound like mom." He laughed pulling her in for a hug. Relief washed over him, he had expected Jenny to put up more of a fight.

King was waiting at the front door, which had been freshly replaced that morning. The sawdust at his feet left his footprints trailing behind him as he swung it open against the plastic sheeting that had consumed the interior of the house. He turned to Grace next to him, reminding her to take it easy as the construction began again at her home.

"Remember, the security team is in full force and they know who the workers are. No one is getting in here without an escort, not in a long shot." He felt guilty that he had to leave them like this. With the burden of a broken home once again resting on Ethan and Grace's shoulders. He was not envious of their predicament. With someone of unknown origin gunning for them and their whole home needing repaired, they should probably be somewhere safer. Unfortunately he wouldn't be able to procure a safe house until he returned to the office to file the paperwork.

"You are going to look into a safe house soon? Right?" It was as though Ethan had read his thoughts. He walked towards the crowd at the door, stopping to wrap his arm around Grace's waist.

"I will. The sooner the better, bud." He had already filled out the forms, he just needed to get the proper signatures and put it through the relocation department. "I'll call as soon as I know anything." King promised with a stout nod of his head meeting Ethan's eyes with concern.

Leaving them alone, even for the drive back to Washington, made him nervous. So much could go wrong. He looked out the front door at the security building down at the end of the drive, hoping they could handle the situation for a day or two while he got things settled.

"Right, thanks." Ethan held out his hand, slapping King on the back as he pulled him in for a handshake, missing the look of dread in King's pleading eyes.

Grace slipped between them with a tight hug, "Take care and drive safe." She whispered. Pulling back, she looked him in the eyes with a smile, faltering when she saw the look of dread washing from his face.

Soon the agents were making their way through the maze of construction tents on the lawn, past the vehicles and security guards, over to Chung's newly returned SUV. He patted it on the hood with appreciation.

"Glad to have you back." He whispered to his key fob as he hit the, now working, beeper. The car unlocked without hesitation and he smiled.

He walked around the black SUV twice before he was satisfied that it was perfectly intact and unarmed. Popping open the trunk, he tossed his bags in. King was still dawdling. Chatting with security on his way through the lawn had slowed him down.

Finally he came rushing out through a tent set up between the vehicle and the house. Hurriedly he tossed his bag on top of Chung's, crushing whatever might have been inside. Chung rolled his eyes, closing the trunk. He spun his keys around his finger while he walked slowly towards the driver side door, beeping the car locked before King could jump in, a jab for making him wait. Chung made a show of taking his time walking towards the front, watching King through the back windows fidgeting as he waited.

With a chuckle, Chung finally unlocked the doors. As he hopped in he barely waited for King to close his door before he had put it into drive and started rolling down the driveway.

Soon the Evans' estate was little more than a speck in the distance.

WAITING

Ethan backed into the house slowly, walking through the plastic curtain that separated the front foyer from the kitchen. Both rooms were under repair, but soon the kitchen would be done and the sheet would keep dust from traveling between the two construction zones. It was like living in a haunted house, the whispering plastic waved in the breezes created by the construction equipment, at night time it was frightening. Hearing the whispers of the plastic caught in unknown breezes, it crinkled throughout the house leaving the impression that hidden predators were lurking unseen throughout the empty house. Ethan reached out to feel the thick plastic, crinkling it in his hands as though hearing the sound in the daylight would make it less alarming. He shuttered at the sound, wondering how much longer they would be safe there.

He stepped farther into the kitchen, waiting for Grace and Jenny to find him. They had stayed outside to watch the car pulling away, although he wasn't sure how they could see through the barrage of tents and vans out in front of the house.

He reached into his pocket pulling out the photograph of him in the fun-house. It was already fraying at the edges. He hadn't let it out of his reach since it had arrived. He held it up to the dim light filtering in from the back window. His face was as pale now as the first time he had found it. It unnerved him that this Colt character knew where he lived. Even more unsettling was the knowledge that he had gained access to the house without passing through the security feeds. Even under the watch of the FBI he had made it into the kitchen to deliver this photograph.

The real question itching at the back of Ethan's mind was, *why?* He had no idea who Colt was, but he had obviously been watching Ethan for years; first sending him after Grace and then his own father.

Why?

Ethan turned the photograph over, holding it up in the light for the umpteenth time, looking for a secret message written in invisible ink, still nothing. Footsteps sounded behind him followed by the crinkling of plastic. He tucked the picture away quickly in his jeans, turning to the front of the house where Grace and Jenny emerged from behind the curtains deep in conversation.

"...but Jen. They are renovating anyway and we have too many. Pick one, it's yours." Grace was still trying to convince Jenny to claim her own room in their sprawling mansion.

Chung had wanted her to stay with Ethan and Grace until he had arranged proper safety measures for her. Suddenly she was involved in this case and as uneasy as he had been to let her get involved, he couldn't just let her go out on her own now. Jenny was in on her brother's secret adventures now and after the last few weeks it would be nice for her to have her own crash pad at their house, somewhere she could feel safe.

"Ethan," Grace turned to him as though he had been chatting with them the whole time. "Jenny should just have a room here, right?" It was a rhetorical question, he knew he didn't need to answer, but she stared at him until he cleared his throat.

"Of course, Chung wants her to stay for a bit and she's always here anyway. Why not have a room of her own." He nodded to Jenny as Grace beamed at him for agreeing with her. "I think there are a couple that aren't under construction right now." He chuckled, "Pick one of them."

"Oh, right." Grace looked to the ceiling, thinking about the damage from the storm while trying to figure out which rooms were still usable. Some had been filled with items from the damaged rooms, but at least two were clear and ready to use.

"Really I don't need my own room, any spare room will do. I can just stay in one of the ones that King and Chung were using. No big deal." Jenny was laughing now, too. Grace was still thinking, stuck like a statue in the middle of the room, staring at the ceiling.

Ethan looked at her for a moment, waiting for her to finish her assessment. Finally she looked back at him, "There are two." She confirmed.

"Perfect." Ethan touched his hand to his pocket feeling for the picture, he wondered how long this room debate would go on for. He had wanted to go through King's notes from the carnival one more time, to learn more about this Colt character. Grace didn't want him involved in the case, but his curiosity was eating a hole in his pocket. He touched the photo one more time, waiting for them to leave.

"Jen, pick a room," Grace begged, "you can keep your stuff in it, even keep spare clothes here... please?"

"Fine, show me the rooms..." Jenny had finally caved.

Although she didn't live far away, she did live out of town. Grace had argued that if the weather was bad it would save her the dangerous drive after work if she had a room at their house. Ethan suspected that she just wanted to keep Jenny close. She had been Grace's only female friend since her escape and had helped Grace to overcome her fear of trusting new people. Jenny had even offered Grace a work placement at her catering company.

"Yay!" Grace cheered, laughing at her ability to negotiate like King.

"Fine, fine, but no pink...? Right...no pink..." Jenny laughed that Grace had finally won the argument. But Grace was already moving on, she had known she would wear Jenny down eventually.

"Do you want the one next to Chung or over by Jerry?" Grace was referring to the two guest rooms that were unused and least damaged by the flood. Although the house was full of many unused guest rooms, only two had remained unscathed by the dripping waters that had consumed most of the lower levels during the storm and with Jenny staying with them for the next while it made sense to settle her into a room that didn't need to be rebuilt. Grace was always practical about the strangest things.

"Let's keep the family together." Jenny shrugged, Grace took her hand and began pulling her to the back stairs to show her new room to her.

Ethan watched like a fly on the wall while they walked through another plastic sheet and off into the house, leaving him alone in the kitchen again. He turned to the fridge, remembering after the putrid smell of decay wafted out to him that it was out of commission. He closed it quickly, eyes watering from the smell and reached for the cooler on the floor, rummaging through for a bottle of water.

He checked back over his shoulder twice before opening the box to retrieve King's notes. They were not the originals, King had taken those with him. These were Ethan's scribbles, things he had read over King's shoulder while he had been filling out his report, things he had heard King saying on the phone, things King had not wanted him to know.

King had only been around for a week after the chaos of the amusement park, before leaving he had spent nearly every waking hour filling in paperwork and chasing leads to get him more information on Colt.

Ethan sat heavily at the plastic covered dining table, setting the small stack of pages on the table before him. He stared at the list, information on Colt that King had amassed through many phone calls. There wasn't much, no first name, no known address, just facts. He had worked for Hart at some point, he was knowledgeable in the fields of electrical and mechanical construction. That last one Ethan had already known, having experienced the carnival firsthand.

Still, Ethan stared at the papers expecting that his short list would explain to him what this man was after and how he could keep his family safe.

When he felt like he could stare at them no longer, he stood to tuck the papers away. The plastic behind him began to crinkle loudly, announcing another presence. He could still faintly hear Jenny and Grace talking on their way up the back staircase, Grace was showing Jenny to the bedroom. He turned slowly, wondering who could be in the house, a chill rolled up his spine as he contemplated the possibilities.

"Gosh darn, this stuff is hard to get through." Jerry commented as he looked towards a startled Ethan across the room, "Oh, how are you?" He asked, watching Ethan with tired eyes.

"Fine," Ethan said, tucking the last of the pages away and quickly closing the box, "you look tired, Jer." He watched Jerry with concern as he crossed the room to join him.

Jerry had just gotten back from visiting Mr. Evans. Ethan could tell by the slouch in his shoulders and the lackluster glow in his eyes. He had taken to visiting Mr. Evans to avoid the construction crews at the house. Jerry wasn't a trusting person and he didn't take well to new faces.

He had a worn frown on his face as he turned to Ethan that didn't come across as progress.

"No, no, just a little tired." Jerry brushed off Ethan's comment as he sat slowly at the table.

Ethan stared at him for a moment longer, dreading the question that pressed familiarly against his lips. "How is he?" Ethan popped off the lid on his bottle of water dropping heavily onto a plastic-clad box as he waited for Jerry to tell him all the details of his father's progress.

Jerry analyzed everything while he was at the hospital, even the look on a nurse's face when he entered the room left him with much to discuss with Ethan. He would watch the numbers on Mr. Evans' beeping machines, slowly learning what was considered good and safe, and what required the attention of the professionals, who would come in running as the screens flashed red.

Sometimes Jerry would explain to Ethan that it had been a malfunction in the equipment, a wire loose, or a sensor becoming unattached. Other times he remained vague with his explanations to Ethan, preferring not to startle him when his father had a rougher day. He was in the best hands there, worrying would do Mr. Evans no good on his path to recovery.

Jerry stood, crossing the room to retrieve a bottle of water for himself, he paced for a moment before settling at the table with a pensive sigh, "His vitals were good today, but no sign of him waking."

Mr. Evans had fallen into a coma three days after being rescued from the amusement park. The strain of his condition had finally become too much for his body to handle, and though he fought it he had finally fallen under so his body could reserve energy for the recovery. That was how the Doctor had explained it to them as they had stood teary-eyed at his bedside. Although he still appeared to be recovering, no one could tell them when or if he would ever wake up.

Not even the barrage of specialists had been able to determine the level of trauma he had been through. In the days he had been awake he had been mostly delirious, rambling on about his childhood and the noises of the carnival. Until he was fully recovered they would never know what he had truly been through in the last fifteen years. Unfortunately, without that knowledge they might not be able to treat him properly.

Ethan had been young when his father had gone missing. After a long period of hopeful waiting, he had been presumed dead. All of his medical records had been destroyed in the aftermath. Now the doctors feared that he had an unknown medical condition that they were unaware of that had led to his coma, like diabetes or something. At least that was what Ethan had overheard them talking about the last time he had visited, he hadn't been back since. There was nothing he could do to help his father recover, but let the doctors and nurses work their magic. He would hate to interfere and have something go wrong.

Even when Jerry went to see him, he just sat still by his bedside, on the other side of the plastic tent they had erected to keep unknown germs from passing between him and the rest of the hospital. To Ethan he looked like a doll wrapped up in plastic. It was too hard to watch his father lying behind a plastic wall looking dead to the world, it reminded him too much of the funeral. His imagination took hold of him when he was in that room and he imagined that his father had looked like this behind the closed lid of his casket so long ago. He shuttered through a sip of water, pushing the thought from his mind with force.

"They said he would regain consciousness when he was ready, Jer. He has a lot of recovering to do..." Ethan quoted the doctor unconvincingly as he sat next to him at the table, shifting over from his spot on the unsteady box. He tried to shake the image of his still father from his mind. "At least his vitals are still doing well." Ethan hoped that the vitals were an indication of how his father was progressing. He liked to imagine that they were his father's way of letting them know that he would be alright, like a secret code that only the sick knew.

Jerry sighed.

"At least he won't have to see his house ripped apart like this."
Jerry looked around the desolate kitchen, "For the second time." He added
as an after-thought. Jerry looked around him at the almost empty kitchen,
flicking his fingers at the plastic wrap that covered it all. "It used to be such
a nice house." He mused quietly to himself.

Ethan chuckled at the thought of his father seeing the house in
such disarray. His father had been gone for so long he had missed all of the
devastating things that had happened to his home. He might never have
known that the house had been abandoned for ten years and demolished
twice. First after a fire Hart had set and then after finally repairing it four
years ago it had brandished the casualties of the storm a week earlier.

At least insurance covered most of it. But by the time Mr. Evans
got back from the hospital the house would be completely new, although it
would look the same Ethan hoped. It had been so long since his father had
been home, he could barely remember what the house had looked like then.
Only that his father had always had a light on in his office, Ethan had
already ventured in to replace the long burnt out bulb in anticipation of his
father's return home. The room had been dark since the bulb burnt out
twelve years ago. Ethan had left it that way, believing that the day the light
went out was the day he would stop mourning his father, it hadn't worked.

MOVING ON

Grace and Jenny had found the spare room, tucked in behind several piles of material for the bathroom across the hall. It had taken them a while to get through the door, moving boxes and piles of wood out of the way to clear a path to get to the doorway. The door hinges creaked in protest, clinging to the pale wooden frame as Grace pried it open before them.

The room was musty and stagnant, although it had remained unscathed by the storm like most of the upper rooms in the house. Grace pulled back the white sheets that covered the furniture, revealing her own four post bed from childhood as a cloud of thick dust billowed into the air beside her. Jenny pulled at the sheets draped around the room piling them on the floor as dust floated up into the air. They made quick work of it, trying to avoid breathing in the clouds of dust that were escaping around the room. Grace stood back quietly, stepping towards the door for a moment when all the furniture was finally uncovered.

"This looks like a little girl's room." Jenny spoke slowly, she picked a teddy bear off of the bed holding it out for Grace to see. Grace crossed the room and took the teddy in her arms, she had forgotten about him since that night on the run when she had last seen him. She smiled as she felt the worn fabric in her hands.

15

"It was mine." She smiled at Jenny. Jenny suddenly understood why this room had been unclaimed before now. This room had been Grace's childhood sanctuary, a place where she could come to escape the life she had with her deranged father.

Jenny knew enough about Grace's broken past to know that Grace had spent a good part of her childhood with the Evans' family. After hearing the things her father had done to her, she understood how important having this safe place had been. She wasn't sure she could take this from Grace, the one place that she had always been safe.

"Are you sure Grace?" She looked to her friend with wide eyes, backing towards the door. She wondered if it would be better for her to take the other room by Jerry.

"No, it's about time this room got revamped. It hasn't been used in fifteen years," Grace walked to the window, pulling back the dusty curtains, "it's time to move on." She smiled back, the sun filtering in behind her lighting the room.

Grace moved to the bedside, pulling back the covers into a pile to be washed.

"I'll get the vacuum." Jenny left the room to give Grace some time in her old room before she had to give it up.

Grace walked around the four post bed, feeling the carved wooden design with her hands, eyes closed, remembering a time when this was the only place she could be free and happy. She remembered hiding in the closet with Ethan and scheming up all kinds of evil childish games and tricks to play on Jerry. She remembered the final hiding place of the evidence she had stolen from her father, hidden behind the secret catch in the closet wall, she wondered sometimes how many secrets this old house still held for her and Ethan to discover, would they find them all? Or would their future children have the pleasure of uncovering the secrets of the

Evans' estate?

She made her way to the closet. It was empty now. Jerry must have taken some time to clean it out when he and Ethan were cleaning the room out to make room for construction. She wondered where it had all gone and thought of checking in storage to see if any of her old things had made their way down there. Perhaps another day she would venture into the crowded wine cellar that had become their storage area looking for remnants of her past.

She held the closet door open, staring at the back paneled wall wondering if Jenny would ever suspect that there was a secret door there. It sure looked inconspicuous. She glanced back over her shoulder, listening for footfalls. The hall was silent. Grace knelt down and tried the trap door one last time, wondering what old secrets it might still be hiding. She felt under the floorboards where she had once stored the files that had led to her father's incarceration and her freedom.

It held nothing now but dust and spiders.

***

Jerry and Ethan had moved their conversation to the front office so they could work. In a silent agreement, they had decided to return Mr. Evans' office to its previous glory before he returned home. It had been stuffed with boxes and memorabilia after the last renovation because it was a room seldom used by anyone in the house and it saved them the extra set of stairs down to the basement with some of the heavier boxes.

Since Mr. Evans' return they had managed to move most of the boxes down to the storage room in the basement. Now that the room was clear they were focusing on finding all of the knick-knacks that had once adorned the shelves behind the cherry wood desk that sat in the center of the room.

"Where is the globe?" Jerry asked over his shoulder as he returned a heavy box of encyclopedias to the shelf behind the desk.

"I think it got moved to the basement, I'll go get it." Ethan raced out the door to retrieve it.

The return of his father had greatly changed Ethan, Jerry had noticed while restoring the front office with him. He had a spring in his step, a lightheartedness that he had lost when his childhood had been pulled from beneath him.

Ethan hopped down the stairwell two steps at a time, excited to see the office returned to its old glory once again. He traced his hand on the wall as he speed-walked through the corridor, smile splayed goofily across his weary face. The damage to the house held little concern for Ethan as he worried himself only with his father's return. The hammering overhead sounded like drums and the saws like his father's humming, he hummed along.

The basement was still musty after the water damage from the storm. He walked past some of the renovation specialists installing their huge dehumidifiers to remove the moisture from the air as he made his way to the back room to find the globe. He tipped his head cheerfully as he passed.

They would have to restore the safe room themselves, it wasn't included in the floor plan and for their own safety it was to remain untold. He had been in to see the extent of the damages before King had left. The supplies had all been packaged in plastic containers, so had been safe from damage, but everything would have to be removed and cleaned thoroughly to prevent mold. It wasn't like the room needed repaired, but cleaning it up would be enough work to keep them busy for a whole week.

He brushed past the secret bookcase, thumbing one of the books with a quiet smile as he turned down the hall to the farthest back room where the boxes were kept.

The storage room was in the farthest back corner of the basement. Originally a wine cellar, it hid behind a large ornate oak door. The shelves, lined with old bottles, were covered in a thick layer of dust, a true testament of how long his father had been gone. It left the room smelling musty with a slight undertone of fermented grapes. Ethan breathed it in deeply, nostalgic as he pressed the thick door open to enter.

With the flick of a switch he was face to face with the tower of boxes that had been removed from the office earlier that week. He knew which one he was looking for, it was labeled "globe". He had known it was from the office when he carried it down, so he had set it aside when he was stacking the other boxes. He picked it up and walked back up the stairs to meet Jerry and see what else was missing.

When he returned to the office he stopped still inside the doorway, an overwhelming elation rolled over him.

"Oh Jerry, it looks just like it used to." He breathed quietly, holding his nostalgia in. He set the box down gently outside the door and walked in. His father's desk was back to its old splendor, with all sorts of global trinkets scattered in his own meticulous order across the front on display. The desk had been dusted and it gleamed in the light filtering through the windows, but the old scratches were still there. Scuff marks from where the chair bumped the desk when he pulled it in, marks from his coffee cup, all the little things that made it look welcoming. It brought back memories of Ethan's father that he had long tucked away for fear of trudging across the memory of the day he had been taken away.

It had been a long October day, Grace hadn't shown up at school. She had called him that morning and told him to meet her before class, but had never shown up. He had been upset that day at her disappearance, unknowing of the fate that had awaited her.

His dad hadn't come home that night, Jerry had remained tense and busy through the evening. He had spent hours on the phone and was too preoccupied to talk to Ethan. Ethan had gone to bed unaware that both his father and Grace would be gone by morning.

The weeks that followed blurred into strobe-light flashes of pain and confusion. His young mind had turned their disappearances into something vivid and horrifying. He hadn't slept for months, waking drenched in sweat as his mind played out the worse scenarios it could imagine. Grace and his father had lived through worse than his mind could have imagined in the years they had been gone, at least he had still had Jerry.

He looked across the room at his old companion and father figure in the absence of his real father. Jerry looked aged and worn after the years of trials they had endured. He had taken Ethan in as his son. Ethan wondered how he was taking Mr. Evans' return in that aspect.

The return of his father, though miraculous, would never replace the years of memories he had stored of Jerry taking him to school, helping with homework and otherwise replacing the father figure he had lost. Jerry had taught Ethan to drive, how to play golf and how to shave. He now looked proudly across the room at Ethan.

"Ethan, you look just like him right now, walking into his office with a new trinket from his travels..." Jerry's eyes crinkled with tears as he walked across the room to retrieve the globe from the box. With a wave of his hand he placed it onto the desk where it had always sat, ready to be spun by Ethan the child any time he asked his father where he had been. "Ta-da." Jerry whispered, stepping back to the door with Ethan to look over their handiwork.

Ethan smiled, placing his hand on Jerry's shoulder.

It finally felt like he was home.

***

As dusk fell, Grace and Jenny finished tidying up the room for Jenny to stay in. It would be a step up from awkwardly sharing a room with her brother. Although he was no longer there to share with, she imagined his grief if she were to be in his space messing up his things. He was a very meticulous person, and liked things in his order. And though it was only a spare room at his friends' home, he had set it up just so before he had left that morning. He would surely know if anyone had entered and ruffled his sheets. Jenny would probably go in there and ruffle them anyway, just to bother him. They might be grown up now, but she still enjoyed picking on him like she had as a child.

"It's all yours now." Grace pulled Jenny in for a hug as she backed out of the room, her work complete.

"Thank you." Jenny whispered after her, still in awe that Grace had been willing to give up her sanctuary.

She stared at the room alone now, Grace and Ethan had gone to pick up some food for dinner. She listened as Ethan's car rumbled down the driveway and off into the night. The room was spacious, no longer frilly, although the walls remained pink with a fading wallpaper trim of roses and ponies. She would let that stay for a while, Grace had seemed reluctant to leave the room when it had been finished. Now it looked plain, simple and livable, the toys and souvenirs from her childhood had been boxed and moved to her new room with Ethan. She would probably go through them on her own time, taking the memories as she could handle them. It would be difficult for her, Jenny felt bad about letting her go through with the room change.

She closed the door behind her as she made her way to the kitchen to set up the table. The chaos of renovating held her attention as she walked through the hall. How marvelous this house had always been, she wondered if it would ever truly be the same after each and every wall was repaired and refurnished. Was it really the same house after all? Or did it feel different to Ethan and Grace when they had had it renovated the last time?

As she wound her way through to the kitchen over the boxes and building supplies she came across Jerry, sitting still in the kitchen. He held a phone up to his ear, she stopped behind the plastic sheet to give him some privacy. He was talking in a hushed voice, it sounded urgent. She leaned in to hear what he was saying,

"Yes, I know," he paused to listen to the muffled sound on the other end, "no I haven't the heart to tell him. He is afraid to come in." It sounded like he was talking to the hospital about Ethan's father, Jenny felt guilty for eavesdropping on something so personal, "Soon, yes, you could call him direct... yes...I know it is his decision, it is his father..." Jenny backed away slowly, giving herself space to make a loud entrance so Jerry wouldn't know she was listening.

It sounded like Ethan's father wasn't doing as well as Jerry had let on, he sounded pained at the thought of breaking the news to Ethan. She didn't envy him the task, telling someone who had just gotten their father back from being presumed dead for fourteen years, just to watching him die a painful death in a hospital where he couldn't even help. She rationed that at least he had gotten to see him again, but given the circumstances, perhaps it would have been better for them both if he really had been dead.

She forged back into the kitchen, stumbling on some of the wood as she tried to announce her presence to Jerry,

"Oohf." She yelled as she stumbled into a sheet of plastic before the entrance to the kitchen, it had caught her off guard in the dim lighting and would have given her away the last time if she hadn't stopped to listen. Some of the plastic sheeting was impossible to see at all until you walked face first into it, she would have to start walking around with her hands out like a zombie if she wanted to stop getting tangled up in it. She plunged through the last of the crinkling plastic with a flourish.

Jerry had finished his phone call, tucking away his cell phone hastily, he greeted Jenny.

"Good evening, Jenny. How is your new room coming along?" He pulled out a chair for her at the dim lit table. Camping lanterns adorned the house on the lower level. Until the electrical was repaired it would remain low lit and much like living in a big camping tent. She slumped down heavily in the chair beside him,

"It's good, I mean, it's a great room..." Her brow furrowed as she listened for Grace and Ethan rustling through the house. When she was sure the area remained still she continued, "I kind of feel bad about taking Grace's old room. It seemed really sentimental to her." She finally whispered across the table. Jerry looked up amused.

"She *had* been holding on to that room," he mused, "she must be ready to get on with it, she seemed really excited to pass it on, you know." He looked at her with knowing eyes.

"Oh," she exclaimed quietly with understanding, "you're sure?" She questioned. He nodded. Behind them the front door slammed, rustling the plastic into ghostly billowing shapes. A moment later Ethan and Grace came fighting their way through with two boxes of pizza,

"Dinner is served." Ethan said. With a small bow he placed the boxes on the table and they all tucked in for some food.

Chatter at the table was minimal that night, with agents King and Chung's absence, the house had been washed with apprehension. Until the agents were back to the field office and had the time to settle the paperwork, they were stuck in a gray zone. Not feeling safe in the house without the agents' protection and not yet able to make the move to a safe house. No one wanted to point out the fact that they were sitting ducks around the kitchen table, anything could happen.

That night they locked and barricaded their doors from the rest of the house. Scraping furniture across the floors and into position it sounded like the house was morphing. When the noise had settled down, Grace heaved a sigh of relief, knowing from the muffled banging that Jerry and Jenny had taken the time to do the same to their own rooms. She felt responsible for them, and if she could have without weirding them out she would have had them all in a room together so she could keep an eye on them. She hadn't been sleeping well with the house so open and insecure. She worried even more now that the agents were gone that they were open to intrusion, Ethan assured her it was her overactive imagination always seeking out the worst that could happen, she worried that he was wrong, and so she had made them all promise to barricade their doors after locking them. Until they were done the construction or in a safe house it was a sure bet that they would be safer that way.

When morning came, rising slow on the horizon, Grace was quick to jump up. Reaching for her phone, she called to the security guard on duty.

"Good morning, how are things Mrs. Evans?" Answered a chipper voice on the other end. Gerard had been head of their security for almost five years now, and was waiting for Grace's morning call.

Given the agents' absence it had made her feel better to get a report first thing in the morning before removing the barricading from her door, and he was nice enough to oblige. This morning she seemed even more nervous than usual as she listened to Gerard on the phone, probably since King and Chung had left the day earlier.

"Very good Gerard, how was the evening?" What she really meant was, *is it safe?* And he knew what to say to appease her mind.

"Clear sailing today Mrs. Evans, clear sailing."

"Thank you, and have a good day."

"And you as well"

The line clicked as Gerard went back to his duties and his morning coffee.

Grace walked to the door slowly, hoping that this morning she could move the barrage of furniture without waking Ethan so he could get a little more sleep. No such luck, as soon as she began to pull at the dresser he hopped out of the bed gently moving her aside to do the heavy lifting for her.

Breakfast was slow, with the kitchen under duress it was more of a drive than anything. Grace and Ethan packed into his car and drove off to town to pick up food for the day and coffee to start the day off. The drive into town was relaxing and quick unlike the rest of the week. On the weekend, traffic generally died down in the mornings when the sleepy stayed in bed.

Grace was anxious, sitting in the passenger seat fidgeting with her hands while Ethan drove the familiar road into town.

"Are you okay?" He finally asked, after she began tapping her feet loudly against the floor mat.

"How long do you think it will take for King to get a safe house for us?" She had been mulling over the thought in her head since they had left the day before, trying to time out how long it would take for their drive, and to get back to the office. She had tried to time it pace for pace, an old habit of hers from her time in the tower. Ethan chuckled at her, pulling into a parking spot, he cut the engine.

"Grace," he began, turning to face her, "they will get us in a safe house as soon as they can, especially with Jenny in the house with us. They would not leave us in that house a minute longer than they had to." He sounded calm and sure of himself, and that was enough to calm Grace's nerves, at least for now.

"I know, I'm just... anxious...I guess." She frowned for a moment, "I just have a bad feeling, that's all." She looked up into Ethan's eyes, embarrassed. "Let's get some food." She declared, opening her door to the light morning air. Ethan followed behind her, worrying about Jerry and Jenny alone in the house, he wouldn't admit it to Grace, but he had had the same odd feeling that something wasn't right.

MOVING OUT

When they returned to the house, a groggy Jenny was waiting for them in the kitchen. Having cleaned out the cooler from the day before, she took the provisions and ice that Ethan was carrying and tucked them into the cold case to keep their food for another day. It was time consuming work, but Grace was unwilling to stay in a hotel. Until they had a safe house, this was it.

Soon Jerry joined them, drawn to the kitchen by the alluring scent of coffee. They sat at the table in silence with a box full of muffins before them, lost in their own thoughts as they filled their stomachs.

A rustling sounded from the front of the house, the front door slammed against the frame. Grace sat stiff in her seat as the others all turned to the hall, waiting to see what was concealed behind the plastic sheeting. The construction crew hadn't arrived for the day yet, Grace was keenly aware.

Ethan stared across the room, doing a head count, they were all at the table. His heart fluttered anxiously as he placed an arm on Grace, standing to place himself between her and the entrance of the kitchen.

With a rustling of the plastic sheet, Gerard entered the kitchen unexpectedly. Grace let out a sigh of relief, relaxing in her chair with a smile.

"Gosh Gerard, you scared me for a moment..." She chuckled as the others relaxed, embarrassed by their fright.

Ethan sat back at the table, relieved that it had only been Gerard.

"Oh, I apologize Miss!" Gerard blushed, forgetting how tense things were in the house now, he wished he had announced his presence better, "Mrs. Evans," he began apologetically, "a letter just arrived. He was a suit, but I thought you would prefer to have it pass through security." He held out a thick envelope in his hand and Grace smiled, taking it from him.

"Thanks Gerard, I appreciate it." She hadn't even noticed anyone out front at the little Security hut when she and Ethan had arrived back at the house, they must have arrived quite recently. She looked at the envelope, wondering what it could contain.

"No trouble." Gerard smiled, "The construction crew is arriving now, I had better go get them signed in..." He nodded to her as he backed through the curtain and out into the front foyer.

Grace handed the envelope to Ethan as she pulled the papers out to look at them. It was a thick stack of papers folded over to fit into the envelope. She opened them up to look. The first page contained an itinerary, and a flight schedule. She passed it to Ethan when she had finished looking it over with wonder, after was a series of plane tickets and a typed note from King, explaining that he would be meeting with them at the safe house after they arrived.

"Wow, he's fast," she commented as she passed the letter over to Ethan. She looked over the plane tickets and frowned, "there are only three here," she turned to Jenny, "you're coming with us right?"

Jenny looked at the tickets in Grace's hands over her shoulder, they were named for Grace, Ethan and Jerry. None were there for her, but she knew her brother had wanted her to stay with them until her apartment was safe, and he hadn't even called yet.

"I thought so." She frowned, hurt that she had been overlooked, Grace looked up at her with worry, knowing that she hadn't a safe place to go to. They couldn't leave her at the house alone, especially in its compromised state, and her own apartment was less safe and had no security detail. Grace stared at the tickets for a minute, knowing that Jenny needed to stay with them to be safe. Maybe Chung had just made her arrangements separately and they just hadn't been delivered yet. Perhaps they had tried to bring them to her at her apartment, thinking she would be there.

"I'll call them and find out what's going on. Yours probably just got sent out wrong," she assured Jenny, "pack your stuff, you're coming with us either way." Then she turned to Ethan, "Show the papers to Jerry, we are leaving tomorrow morning, he'll want to get ready."

"Yeah." He passed the corresponding letters over to Jerry, who was peering over his shoulder eagerly waiting to see their destination. He pulled his reading glasses up to his face to study the itinerary for the next day. When he was finished he placed the pages on the table for the others to continue looking over.

Standing slowly he left the room through a rustling breeze of plastic, "I had better find some luggage, I think it's in storage..." he called over his shoulder as he walked away whistling into the empty hallway.

"I won't miss that." Grace laughed after him, looking back to the page over Ethan's shoulder for a number to contact, "ooh, looks like we are going to Florida." She smiled as she scanned the page over. "I hope there's a pool!"

Ethan passed her the papers so she could get a better look at the contact information. "Wait up Jerry." He called as he followed Jerry out of the kitchen to help him on his quest to find some luggage in their crowded storage room.

Grace stared at the papers for a moment longer knowing that Jenny was watching her impatiently, wondering what her own fate would be. Grace continued searching for a number until she finally found it, tucked into the back of the last page.

She set the paper on the dusty counter, and pulling out her phone she dialed. It rang for several minutes before disconnecting with her abruptly. She looked at the number again, it specified to text. *Odd*, she thought. Opening a message, she requested a ticket for Jenny Chung, detailing that she was staying with them until her home was secured. A moment later her phone pinged with a generic message stating that Jenny's ticket would be waiting for them at the counter.

She waived her phone at Jenny across the room triumphantly, "Get packing lady, you aren't getting rid of me that easy." Jenny smiled, trying to hide her relief. She wasn't ready to be alone at her apartment just yet, and though she hadn't admitted that to her brother she had thought he would know her well enough after knowing her for her whole life to know that. He was going to get a talking to the next time she saw him for sure.

"Thanks Grace." She handed over a paper cup of coffee, "I'll have to go to my place to get my passport and stuff."

"You don't need one, it's not international," Grace waived the paper at her like it was proof.

"Right, I guess I'll get packing then, I'm living out of a suitcase anyway, shouldn't be too hard." She picked up her cup and walked off to gather her things, stumbling through the covering with wild waiving arms, nearly spilling her coffee as she went. She called back to the kitchen, "I'm not going to miss this plastic either!" Grace laughed loudly from the kitchen.

Grace found herself wandering towards the basement storage, so she wouldn't be left alone on the main floor as the construction crew began entering. She found Ethan and Jerry in the old wine cellar rummaging through the boxes in the back. She leaned on the door for a moment watching them, trying to figure out where they had tucked the luggage before she let them know she was there.

"Hey fellas how it going?" She called in, as they shuffled over another set of boxes.

Ethan peeked his head out from behind the stack, "Grace? Is that you?"

"Yeah, just checking up on the two of you. Any luck yet?" She asked as she made her way in towards him, knowing that once she announced her presence she would be obligated to help search.

"Jerry thinks they are somewhere in the back." Ethan frowned as Grace reached his position. They had stacked the boxes to save space, not to make them easily accessible. She supposed they should have thought it over, knowing that they would be going to a safe house sometime soon when they had moved the storage down there earlier in the week.

"Let's get to it then." Grace wanted to sound encouraging, but she was too worn from the weeks of trials and worry, it came out more like a whimper.

Soon Grace and Ethan were moving the boxes to make a pathway towards the back of the room where Jerry had told them the luggage was hidden. Jerry had gone back upstairs to make arrangements with security and collect his personal items.

Jerry, unlike Grace and Ethan, had never been sent to a safe house before. So while Grace and Ethan knew what amenities would be available to them, Jerry felt as though he was required to pack up his whole life. He had seemed flustered when he had left, trying to recall what he wanted to pack and what he needed to bring.

Jerry was just packing the last of his medications into his bag when Jenny knocked on the door.

"Hey, Jerry, are you busy?" She stood in the door frame looking flustered as he zipped up his carry on.

"Not at all, what's the trouble?" He asked, watching her face as she frowned deeper.

"I'm just not sure what I need to bring." Jenny spoke quietly, and Jerry sensed that she was as nervous as he was about their unexpected travels.

Jenny had only a small duffel bag with her, and it comprised mostly of the clothing she had packed in her haste to reach the house a week earlier, only a couple of outfits and a set of pajamas. She didn't want to leave with only one spare set of clothes, but was nervous about traveling on her own to her empty apartment. Jerry had a solution.

"Why don't we go see Gerard and see if one of the security guards will accompany you to your apartment so you can get your things?" Jerry was very practical in his observation, Jenny's face lit up with excitement.

"Oh that's a great idea, thanks." She left quickly and within a few minutes Jerry could hear her car starting. Grace wouldn't be too pleased that he had allowed Jenny to leave, he hoped she would understand.

***

Ethan and Grace arrived at Jerry's door a moment later, luggage in hand.

"Where did Jenny go?" Grace's face was white as a ghost as she stared at Jerry with concern.

"I told her to bring a security guard," he nodded to show that he had spoken with Jenny before her departure, "she needed some things from her place."

Grace sighed with relief, "Thank you Jerry." She carried an empty luggage bag into his room and placed it on his bed next to the neatly folded pile of belongings he had amassed to bring with him.

"Do you need any help with that?" She asked as she unzipped the luggage, flapping it open across his bed.

"No, thank you. You and Ethan should go and get your things ready."

"Alright, let me know." She nodded again, before disappearing down the hall with Ethan, the rolling wheels of their luggage trailing behind them.

They wouldn't have to leave until early the next morning, but spent most of the day packing and locking up the house, eager for their departure. Many of the rooms wouldn't need to be accessed by the restoration company, so Grace took the large ring of keys for the interior of the house and walked room to room, looking them over and locking them up.

She called Gerard again, to let him know of their plans, so he could minimize the staff while they were away. It would give them a chance to take a break, maybe cover some vacation time. They had been busy over the last few weeks, more so than normal, and Grace hoped that they would take some time to wind down while the house was empty.

The day passed quickly, in a flash they were back in their rooms barricading the doors for the last time. By the time night fell they were all settled in with alarms set for before dawn to wake them to get to the airport.

TAKE OFF

King drove through the night. Much to Chung's displeasure, he had called for a rest stop the night before to kick the stomach flu that he had caught on the way out of town. It had delayed them a full day, now with only a few hours to go, King was behind the wheel while Chung had his turn at the bug.

Chung had insisted that King keep driving so he could finish his sickness in his own apartment.

A retching sound came from the back seat as Chung emptied his stomach for the fifth time in as many minutes, he cursed from the back seat,

"You mind slowing down?" He whined to King as his stomach turned again.

"Sure thing." King smiled unapologetically, pressing his foot to the petal. Chung would thank him when he got home faster and had a chance to sleep. King rolled down the window to let in some fresh air to wash away the stagnant sick smell that was slowly taking over the back seat. Chung was going to kill him if he couldn't get the smell out of his baby, the car that is. He had just gotten it back.

The roads grew quieter as the night progressed, soon the busy interstate was down to them and a truck and their cut-off was fast approaching.

Chung had finally fallen asleep in the back, shivering from fever. King called gently over his shoulder, "Almost there, buddy," the back seat began to stir, so King continued, "I'm staying at your place tonight, no chance you can drive me back to my place like that." He looked into the rear view mirror in time to see Chung reaching for a bag. "Yeah, I thought you might say that." He joked, pulling off the highway and into the suburbs.

He slowed as they reached the apartment building, fumbling with Chung's car keys for the key fob that would gain him entrance to the underground parking. Chung was alive in the back seat, moaning and grunting as he thought longingly of his warm bed upstairs. Before King had parked, he was out the door and racing for the elevator.

"I'll get the bags, don't worry." King muttered to himself as he tried to find Chung's reserved parking space. It took him a few minutes to get their luggage up the stairs to the elevator. By the time he reached Chung's apartment, his partner was already in the washroom. He had left the door open a crack, inviting King in as he had raced for the toilet. King didn't envy him, it had been a horrible flu bug. He wondered if Ethan and the others had caught it, or if they had picked it up on their way back.

King locked the door behind him and settled himself on the couch for the night, leaving their luggage scattered across the front entranceway. He was tired, it could wait.

***

Jenny awoke with a start as the beeping of her phone dragged her away from her sweet dreams. A thumping down the hall indicated Grace and Ethan were already up and getting ready. She wearily pulled back the covers to get ready for the day.

She dressed quickly, but by the time she had reached for the deadbolt the rolling sounds of luggage were already sounding outside her door.

"Are you ready, Jenny?" Grace called from the other side of the door with her suitcase trailing behind her. Her excitement shone through her tired voice. For Grace this was a vacation, Jenny couldn't help but feel bad for her again. The simplest things in life had eluded Grace, she hadn't had the chance in her life to just fly away for a vacation. She might have gotten her freedom back, but to the rest of the world she had still lived like a prisoner for the last few years. With all the chaos surrounding her escape, this might be the first chance she had to just get away somewhere nice and put it all behind her. Jenny sighed.

"Yeah, I'm ready." Jenny called back out as she pulled at the doorknob. With her small duffel bag in hand, she stepped into the hall to give Grace a morning smile, "Coffee on the road then?"

Grace nodded with a smile and turned to pull her luggage back to the front of the house.

By the time Jenny and Grace had reached the front doors, Ethan was heading back up the stairs to take their luggage down to the car. His and Jerry's were safely in the trunk of his car already.

Jerry sat in the passenger seat, waiting with a pair of sunglasses and a goofy sun hat, at least he hadn't lost his sense of humor. He waved out of the window cheerfully,

"Are you ready for some sun?" He called to Grace and Jenny as they walked down the steps. Grace laughed, pulling his goofy hat off of his head through the window, she put it on her head and stared back at him.

"I am now..." She giggled, posing with his hat before returning it to his head and climbing into the back seat after Jenny. For an early morning, they were all in good spirits, glad to leave the mummified house behind them for a while and forget about their worries.

At three in the morning, the car pulled out of the Evans estate, Grace looked back over the seat to watch as it faded into darkness. All of the lights were out, save the flashing reds of the security cameras. Gerard waved to them as they passed his gate.

"Have a safe trip, see you when you get back." He called. Even Gerard wasn't privy to the knowledge of their destination, he just knew that they were going away for a while. It was the whole point of being in a safe house, only those on the inside knew.

Once Jenny was there she wouldn't be leaving until the rest of them did. Grace hadn't told her yet, she worried that Jenny would react badly if she realized that her brother wouldn't need to put up surveillance at her apartment, rather she would be cast away with Grace and the others until the danger passed. Maybe that was his plan the whole time. It would save him time and about three weeks' worth of paperwork.

Jerry leaned back over his seat, "Can you figure this out Grace?" He passed back the GPS and a slip of paper with the address for Blue Grass Airport in Lexington. She smiled and took them both.

"Sure thing."

Grace looked down as she typed in the address. The touch screen on the GPS shaking in her excited hands made it difficult for her fingers to find the letters. Finally she took a deep breath and tried one last time. As the destination loaded up, Grace looked it over. It would take two hours to get to the airport if traffic was good. Their flight left at six, they would have plenty of time when they got there to go through security and have a coffee. She passed it back to Jerry a moment later.

"Thanks." He pressed it back into the dashboard for Ethan to see.

Grace leaned back in the seat next to Jenny, watching as the dark sky began to glow on the horizon. Soon the stars were melting away into the encroaching light. Grace watched the sunrise swallow up the last lingering twinkle on the horizon. She had watched enough sunrises in her life to know that today it brought good weather. A light breeze trickled in through Ethan's window as he opened it a crack to let in some cool air to keep him awake in the early morning hours. Before Grace could watch the rest of the darkness fade away they had arrived.

Ethan pulled in to a far back corner before parking. Hopping out of the car he took a minute to stretch himself back out, "Oh my legs." He muttered to himself before walking around the back to pop the trunk. Sitting in the car for so long had left them all stiff. Grace and Jenny stretched out as they walked to the trunk to help with the bags. They pulled out their luggage and walked to the shuttle stop to wait for a bus to the front gates.

The bus was small and cramped, it smelled like shoes and wet dog, but Grace supposed it could have been worse. It took them to the front gates in shaky jerking motions, like it was on its last leg. When they arrived Ethan took Jerry's bags for him, leaving his aging hands free to carry their tickets, they approached the front desk to retrieve Jenny's ticket and pick their seats.

The line passed quickly at the front counter, and soon they all had seats and boarding passes, unfortunately none of them would be sitting together,

"I guess we should have been earlier, it's been so long since I've flown." Jerry looked at his ticket with a frown.

"That's fine, we're all going to the same place anyway." Grace commented as Jerry passed over her ticket. He passed Jenny and Ethan theirs after checking over the names and seat numbers like he was trying to memorize them.

"We should get to the gate then." Jenny pointed down the crowded corridor ahead of them, shaking her flimsy ticket towards another line. The security check line looked long and slow, it would take them a while to get through. They weaved slowly through the crowd with their carry-on bags in tow.

The security line was longer and slower than it had looked from down the hall, by the time they were through they had to race to make it to their gate in time for takeoff. Grace's stomach rumbled as she raced past a small airport bakery. She thought longingly of the food she had hoped to have before the flight. They were the last to board the plane, as they rushed to take their seats the attendant began her welcome speech. Grace paid extra attention, she had loved flying as a kid. She waited for the flight attendant to go through her whole safety speech with the pamphlet open in front of her, amused by the small drawings and diagrams before her.

It was a small plane carrying no more than thirty. Grace found that odd. Florida was a popular destination, normally it would be a much larger plane. She watched out the window as the plane began moving to the runway, reaching into her purse she popped out a piece of gum to prevent her ears from popping and to appease her growling stomach. Ethan sat across the aisle from her. She passed him over a piece and sat back with her eyes closed.

Soon they would be safe.

DEVIATION

King awoke early to the sound of Chung retching in the bathroom, he would probably be staying home sick. King called for a cab while he walked into the hall, grabbing his bags. He couldn't take the day off, he needed to get the paperwork in for the safe house. He had promised Ethan it would be in yesterday and their safety was hanging in the balance. Chung would understand. As he hopped into the cab he checked his phone, a voicemail from Ethan. He deleted it, they were probably wondering when the paperwork was going to be ready. He would call him back from the office as soon as it was signed, it should only take a few minutes if he called in a few favors. He could probably have them out of the house and settled by the next day.

The office was in an uproar when he arrived five minutes later, the files had arrived from the case he and Chung had taken on during their vacation. He waved his way through the banter and pats on the back, walking straight to the supervisor's office with his paperwork. He knocked on the open door before entering.

"Good morning sir." He nodded to the man behind the desk. Agent Clark was an aging man of good humor, he looked up and smiled at King.

"Couldn't take a break, could you?" He laughed, waving at a pile of folders scattered across his desk.

"No Sir, I never slow down." King sat heavily in the vacant chair, placing his papers on the desk between them, "Can you sign these? I need a safe house for the Evans again, until this case is closed." He pushed the paper forward to Clark.

"Sure thing, get them outta there today. I hear the house is a mess again?" Clark knew all about the Evans' previous ordeal, he had been involved in their last case against Hart.

"Yes sir, it's a wreck. Chung's sister Jenny is there as well, do you think we should send her with them?" He had been wondering the whole drive down if Jenny would be safe on her own at her apartment, he hadn't asked Chung, he didn't think he was worried. He should be, Jenny was now just as much a target as the others and being a relative she would be a likely target to keep agent Chung away from pursuing the case. If she was involved, he would be compromised. Clark seemed to get the same impression, he reached for a pen scribbling a few notes on the page before signing it.

"Send her with them." He agreed, sliding the pages back towards King. It was done, now he just needed to make the arrangements and they would be on their way. Behind him a knock sounded on the still-open door,

"Sir, oh good you're here too, welcome back King." Agent Balek stood in the open door with pursed lips, "Got a flag, Grace and Ethan Evans just boarded a plane, are they going to a safe house?" He peered over King's shoulder at the paperwork with a frown. King stood suddenly.

"Not yet they aren't," He quickly crossed the room to pull the pages from Balek's hand, "Florida? Why are they going to Florida?" He looked at his phone, kicking himself for deleting the message Ethan had sent, it was probably an explanation. Instead he dialed Chung. The phone went straight to voicemail so King left him a message.

"Chung, get your ass outta the bathroom and call me back, Ethan and Grace are on the move. Something's wrong." He hung up, pulling the passenger manifesto out of the pile of pages that Balek had been carrying. He scrolled down the short list, frowning, "Chung's sister was on the flight, and Jerry..." He paused looking it over again, "Shit." He muttered, looking to agent Clark for advice.

"Looks like you're going to Florida, King." Clark stood from behind his desk, "Get it organized, no going in guns blazing this time." He followed the two agents out of his office into the main room to make the announcement.

***

Jenny hated flying. She was seated at the back of the plane away from the others, and out the window she could see the clouds. With a deep breath she pulled down the blind, blocking out the view. Beside her a man chuckled, his large brown eyes crinkled at the edges.

"Not much for flying are you?" He smiled at Jenny sincerely.

"No, not really, sorry." She looked at her knees, breathing in deeply.

He waived to the attendant in the aisle, "Water." He whispered, she nodded at him. Soon she was at the edge of his seat with a plastic cup of water, he passed it to Jenny,

"Thanks." She nodded towards the attendant.

"My name's Jake." The man beside her smiled.

"Jenny." She said, bringing up her hand to take a drink.

"Well Jenny, you know what keeps me from being a nervous flier?" He stared at her with a smirk, "Talking to the pretty lady beside me." She laughed, choking on some of the water while she tried to catch her breath.

"What are you going to Florida for?" She asked, curious at his outgoing demeanor, her nerves had already begun to calm. She thought maybe if he kept talking it would distract her from the height.

"Wedding." He nodded, shaking his head when he looked up at Jenny's confused expression, "No, no, not *my* wedding, I'm the best man..." He smiled even wider. "How about you?"

Jenny sipped on her water for a moment, to avoid answering his question. She had never been in a position like this before and wasn't sure what she should say. She couldn't tell him she was going to a safe house, what if someone on the plane overheard. She thought about it for a moment longer.

"Vacation." She said finally, thinking of Grace and her excitement to get away somewhere sunny for a while.

"Ah, nice choice." He bantered on, Jenny finally felt her muscles relaxing, as she engaged in conversation with the man beside her and forgot about her worries.

Jenny listened as Jake told her his friend's romantic idea, why they were flying down early to surprise the bride on her big day. It sounded so sweet, and Jenny couldn't help but think what it must be like to have someone care that deeply for their partner. She smiled at Jake's jokes and wished she had the courage to say more to him.

***

Chung wiped off his chin and placed his toothbrush back on the counter. He could hear his phone beeping from the kitchen. Groggily he walked to it, pulling his sweater tight and zipping it on his way.

He picked it up off of the counter, a message from King flashed on the screen. He held it up to his ear expecting to hear that he had missed out on a celebratory cake. As the message played out he frowned. Keys in hand, he was out the door before the message had finished playing.

In less than five minutes he was walking through the office door, right into the middle of Clark's address.

"...and in addition to Mr. And Mrs. Evans, in this particular case the civilians Jenny Chung and Jerry Smith are also to be removed into protective custody." He looked across the room meeting eyes with Chung as the door swung closed behind him, his mouth gaped open in horror. Quickly he righted himself, staring stoically back across the crowd of agents ready to continue his address.

"My SISTER is out there?" Chung marched through the room stopping an inch from King's nose, "You didn't mention Jenny..." He fumed, staring his partner in the eyes. King looked down at his feet shamefully.

"I didn't check the passenger manifesto until after I called. I didn't think you would find out like this..." King whispered apologetically, the whole room was watching and he could feel a flush creeping over his face.

Chung turned sharply, meeting agent Clark's eyes with fury.

"Go on." He snipped, standing still as he waited for the rest of the information King had failed to tell him.

Clark paused for a minute, holding eye contact with Chung, while he waited for the agent to stop fuming. He continued slowly, treading cautiously as Chung watched him impatiently.

"The team has been selected, you will be heading out shortly. Please look over your information packages while in transit." He pointed to a stack of folders that had been placed beside him by one of the other agents. King stepped forward to retrieve two, handing one to Chung with an apologetic look of condolence.

"Let's go." Chung tucked the folder under his arm and began marching towards the door. King waited in the office behind him. Before he had reached the door, Chung was racing back, tossing his folder haphazardly at King as he sped to the washroom.

"This is gonna be rough..." King muttered to himself.

TURBULENCE

Grace stared across the aisle and out the window past Ethan and his seat companion, watching as the clouds passed underneath. With a small jolt she felt as though her heart had stopped momentarily, she turned to look out the window on her side. The sky was clear, save a few scattered fluffy clouds.

The plane jolted again, Grace grabbed for the armrest as she stared down the aisle at the flight attendants. They had gathered at the front of the plane and seemed to be in deep discussion about something.

The passengers on the plane were quiet, Grace hated to whisper to Ethan across the aisle, but the flight attendants were acting strange, rushing around with wide eyes, looking at the passengers with remorse. Grace was confused when the plane shook again, catching her breath in her throat.

"Ethan." She called to him in a hushed voice, tapping his arm across the aisle. He looked to her with wonder, "What's going on?" She stared at the attendants, trying to divert his attention to their sporadic behavior. He leaned into the aisle to look at the attendants, his brow furrowed while he followed their movements.

"I don't know." He whispered back. He continued to stare at the front of the plane where they were converging outside the door to the pilot room. "It doesn't look good." He held her hand tightly for a moment to reassure her while he continued to watch the attendants with concern. Overhead the seatbelt warning pinged for the tenth time in three minutes.

Grace squeezed his hand back, turning away from the attendants to look at the view from her window. She frowned, looking out the window past the man beside her. The plane was low in the sky. She could see the waves breaking off the coast. The plane began to shake, Grace grabbed for the armrest, holding it tightly as the plane jerked forward. Suddenly her stomach was in her throat, the seat beneath her vanished as the plane began falling, the belt held her in place as she gripped the armrest in protest.

"Ethan!" She called across the aisle with panic, she looked to him, holding onto his own armrests. He was staring forward with horror, Grace looked back to the front. She saw that the luggage compartments were opening, dispelling parcels across the plane. A bag landed heavily on her shoulder as the oxygen mask popped down in front of her, smacking her in the face. She reached for it with one hand, clinging to the armrest with the other, holding on for her life. She pulled it over her head as the world became fuzzy. Grace closed her eyes, focusing on breathing as the loose luggage on the plane battered against her. She clung tight.

***

Ethan watched out the window as the Gulf of Mexico came rushing at him. It seemed to happen instantaneously, as he floated from his seat the plane crashed into the water, behind him he could hear an explosion of metal. He closed his eyes, mask in hand, anticipating the rush of water. Instead he landed in his seat with a thud, knocking the wind out of him. His eyes opened and he looked for Grace, she was beside him, reaching for his hand. He took her outstretched palm and wrapped his hand in hers.

Passengers were scrambling towards the front of the plane where an emergency door had been opened. Grace and Ethan were caught up in the surge as water began pooling at their feet. He clung to her hand, knocking back anyone who dared to come between them. Beyond the planes gaping doors were crashing waves and glaring sun, it took a moment for Ethan's eyes to adjust. With a shove from behind, he and Grace slid off the inflatable ramp and into the chill water.

His breath caught in his throat as he momentarily let Grace's hand go, he reached for her as the splashing around him became frantic. Wasn't there supposed to be an inflatable boat or something at the bottom of the slide? He had always thought that was how it was supposed to happen, movies had led him to believe that when a plane crashed there would be a boat.

His brain was foggy, flashing before him as he tried to absorb his surroundings. Grace grabbed him by the hand pulling him towards her and away from the frantic frenzy of the splashing passengers. By the time he could see the island, Grace was already tugging him by the arm towards it.

He splashed in the water, fighting the urge to swim against the crashing waves as he tried to keep Grace's hand in his. She was a good swimmer and had turned onto her back to pull him along behind her. A wave crashed over his head as he struggled to stay afloat. The world went dark.

SEPARATION

Jerry sat pensive in his seat, watching the flight attendant as she reached for the pilot phone. Her face did not hide her worry. He looked out the window, acutely aware of their diminishing altitude. Pulling his belt tighter, he listened as she spoke to the pilot wide eyed, hearing only snippets of her half of the conversation, "Yes...no...really?...what should we do??" With one look to Jerry, she sat beside him and buckled herself in tightly.

"Hold on sir, it's an emergency landing." She whispered, not having enough time to alert the rest of the passengers as the plane began to buck in the air. She placed her hand on his for comfort as he stared out the window with worry. With a popping sounded, masks fell from the overhead compartment. He peeled his eyes from the window long enough to cover his face as the plane crashed.

His ears were buzzing from the sudden drop in altitude, his hands fumbled with his buckle as the plane dipped slowly on the water. He pulled himself to his feet after a gentle tug from the flight attendant. She reached towards a lever in the wall, gently pushing him out of the way as she tugged open the emergency exit. She pressed her hand into his back, talking to him in a language he couldn't understand over the ringing in his ears. She was pointing urgently out of the door, pressing firmer into his back. He began walking forward into the light of the outside world.

Water swirled in at him making his progress difficult as the passengers pressed him farther away from the door. With one step the world slipped out from beneath him, he was suddenly falling into the depths below, it seemed to take forever, but the chilly splash at the bottom nearly knocked the wind out of him

He splashed to the bottom of the small slide, crashing into the deep with others flailing beside him, dragging him down. He kicked them off, struggling to right himself and get his bearings as he splashed away from the plane and into the Gulf of Mexico with nothing to keep him afloat but his own aging limbs.

He floundered, trying to right himself long enough to catch his breath as waves came rushing towards him. Finally, popping up like a cork from under a rolling mass of salt water, he managed to stay afloat treading water.

That was when he saw it, ahead of him in the waves, like a beacon of hope just barely visible on the horizon above the crashing water; an island. The lush green of the trees instilled hope as he struggled against the salty chill of the waves around him.

Behind him, the glare of the morning sun cast a glow on the cresting waves. He dove into the water, holding his breath as he pressed towards the shoreline, when he popped out of the water he saw it more clearly. Small and desolate, it was cut off from the rest of the world. It was probably a private island owned by some rich executive with nothing better to buy, it would probably have a satellite phone or radio somewhere.

He didn't even care at that point, getting anywhere safe was his only instinct. Help would arrive once they discovered that the plane was down, he was sure of that, but he knew that he wouldn't be able to survive in the water much longer, none of them would. He scanned the water looking for others as he treaded the water beneath him. With no yellow life raft in sight, swimming to the island seemed to be his only hope for survival.

He set the island ahead of him, fighting with every ounce of energy he had to combat the waves as they tried to pull him back out to the sinking plane, he didn't look back. Behind him he could hear the screams subsiding, replaced by floundering splashes as the other passengers kicked into survival mode, fighting to get ashore before they drowned.

He broke through another wave and his feet finally touched the bottom, he trudged towards the brown sand with renewed reverence. Behind him the splashing and shouting grew louder, other passengers were beginning to reach the shoreline as well.

Suddenly Jerry realized he was alone, turning towards the wreck he held his hand up to shield the strong morning sun from his eyes. Out there in the waves were his family. He watched as each passenger passed him by, ignoring their offers to help him, he would wait until he found Grace and Ethan.

Across the crashing waves, he caught a flash of red hair, he rushed out towards it hoping it was Grace bobbing in the ebbing tide. A hand smacked him in the face as he tried to reach out to the red headed floating body. It was Ethan, struggling to hold his head up above the water. Jerry smiled, and threw his arm around Ethan's waist, letting his feet find the bottom so he could stop kicking frantically. He smiled, pulling Jerry in for a wet hug.

With a tug on her arm, Grace looked up. Seeing that the others were standing, she let her feet drift towards the ground.

Together they fought their way to shore.

When they had reached the water's edge, soaked and shivering, Grace turned to look at the plane sinking slowly beneath the crashing waves. *How had this happened?* She wondered, looking across the beach at the other wet passengers that had already splashed their way to shore. The water was still alive with frantic swimmers, fighting against the massive waves that were trying to pull them back out to the wreckage.

A movement caught her eye, she stared into the sun watching as a large object moved from behind the plane. Her heart leapt into her throat when she realized, the awful grinding metal sound she had heard as they crashed into the water was the back end of the plane separating. It had caught a current, tail end up, it floated around the island and out of view. She raced across the beach trying to keep it in view as she shouted desperately into the wind.

"JENNY!" She called over the crashing of the waves, but it was too late.

SURVIVAL

Chung was raiding the bathroom supply closet for something to combat the remaining symptoms of his flu bug, he wasn't about to step back and hand this one over with his own sister in peril. A knock at the door told him King was back with some medicine.

"Here, this should do." King passed over a bag filled with medications, allowing Chung to take his pick of the lot.

"When are we heading out?" He asked over a glass of water, downing a concoction of the pills at once.

"Fifteen minutes. They have a team in Florida waiting at the airport to secure them when they land. Should be a quick one, and then they are off to a safe house." King looked Chung over with worry, he looked deathly pale, and he shook like a leaf as he washed some water over his face.

"Let's go." His voice had more determination than his face showed.

The small group of agents walked through the door with set faces, Chung would never know how important it was to them to keep his sister safe. He was their family and they would do anything for their family. Jenny was about to get the saving of a lifetime.

Silently they piled into a black van, destination; the airport tarmac. The van pulled them straight up to the jet, they had no need for customs and security, because they *were* security. The jet took off with a whirring speed, pressing Chung back into his seat as his stomach churned. He hoped the worst of his sickness had passed as the jet reached its altitude and his ears popped.

He listened while they sped through the air, waiting for a call that the plane had landed and they had been found safely, the call never came. With a last look out the window and a frown, they were landing in Florida. A team of twenty waited on the runway with stone faced stares as the approaching jet slowed before them.

Chung's stomach churned again, this time it wasn't from the flu.

As the jet coasted to a stop, he jumped from his seat, rushing out the door with the others who had already seen the looks on the waiting agents' faces.

"This doesn't look good." King held Chung back a moment, steadying him before letting him join the crowd.

"I know." Chung replied, pressing his way into the crowd with determination.

The others approached with caution, not sure which of the agents before them was the sibling of Jenny, finally their lead agent spoke as the roaring of the jet subsided behind them.

"The plane has made an unexpected landing, off course, near Big Pine Key." He looked across the waiting faces as he addressed them, backing away from Chung when he realized from the fury crossing his features that he was the brother of the endangered Jenny. "We are working with the air authority to pinpoint the crash...uh...landing site." He corrected himself, watching Chung's features as he continued, still backing away from the approaching agent, "We should have a more accurate location within a few hours, and in the meantime we are coordinating efforts to move a rescue team to Big Pine Key to await further instruction." He looked up at King pleadingly as he anticipated retaliation from Chung who was pacing inches from his face. With a glare, Chung stopped pacing.

"Let's get moving then." Chung walked into the airport proper, following the direction of the lead agent to enter a small board room. He glanced back at the runway wondering how long it would be for their transport to arrive, every minute that they waited was a minute of his sister's life hanging in peril. Then there were Ethan, Grace and Jerry, he hadn't taken the time to think of them. His heart stopped as he crossed the threshold into the board room, knowing that Jenny had others with her, others that he had sworn to protect. A thick wave of guilt washed over him, he passed an apologetic look to King. He hated to put his partner in a position like this.

Chung stood still with guilt while the teams reviewed their procedures in the small crowded room. He stood with his back to the wall by the door, ready to run if his stomach began churning again, he felt a different kind of sick now. Guilt washed over him, he worried about Jenny and his rage was flaring up at the thought of her in peril. He knew he would have been worried if it was just Grace and Ethan, but putting his sister into the mix stirred up a force inside him that was worth reckoning with.

He felt adrenaline coursing through his veins, he stared at the small table, knowing if given the chance he would rip it in half and toss it across the room, maybe smash a window, he held it in. But if they didn't hurry this thing up and get to them soon, he was going to lose it.

***

Jenny watched in horror as the front of the plane disappeared, dipping the seats ahead of her into the water, she held to her seat tightly, while the tail of the plane tipped into the air. She could feel herself falling forward into the seat ahead of her, the mask at her face pulled as she leaned forward. She could see the lifeless bodies floating in the water beneath her. Beside her Jake had pulled his buckle off and climbed across the aisle to find an exit, using the seat backs like steps. She paid little attention to him, her body remained frozen in her seat watching with horror as the scene before her burned itself into her mind. Was this the last thing she would ever see? Grace, Ethan and Jerry flashed into her head. Were they already under water, was she the only one left breathing? Her heart raced as Jake fumbled with the seat backs behind her.

"Jenny!" He called into the echoing cabin, water began circling closer. She turned to look, he was holding out a hand for her, gently guiding her to the back of the plane where he had found a way out. His voice echoed in the underwater cabin, sounding distant in her buzzing ears as the frozen shock washed from her body suddenly.

"Hang on." Jake called to her, lifting her as he stumbled over the seat backs. She took one last fleeting glance towards the rising water, pushing the thought of the others quickly out of her mind.

She reached for her buckle, holding his hand firmly as she released it, the release slammed her suddenly into the seat back in front of her as it let her go. Jake grimaced as she nearly tugged him down with her.

Following his lead, they climbed upwards towards the back of the plane. She could feel it sink below them as it sucked in water, they reached the opening at the same time.

"Ladies first." Jake gave her a light shove towards the opening. She stared at the raging water beneath her, the sinking plane was sucking water in around it. She knew that she need to get as far away from the water vacuum as she could, or she would be sucked back in.

With a knowing nod, they both dove as far from the departing plane tail as they could and into the fast approaching water.

Jenny hit the surface with a resounding smack, knocking the air from her, she fought not to suck in a breath while under the chill water. Her muscles tensed in defiance as she struggled to right herself. She opened her eyes to the darkness around her unsure which way was up in the chaotic swirl of the water around her, panicking she began to kick her legs praying that they would take her in the right direction.

As she bobbed to the surface, she gasped, relieved that she had made it. Her lungs ached from holding her breath for so long, a wave splashed over her head as she fought to tread water in the chaotic current. She looked for Jake, finally he called to her over the crashing waves.

"Swim towards the island, stick together."

She spun around looking for the island, finally seeing it as a wave rose her above the tide with it. It was quite a distance away, she took a deep breath wondering if she could make it that far. She glanced back for a second to find Jake in the water, keeping him close, she started to swim.

"Got it!" She called back, setting the island in sights. It was a small island she imagined it was probably private, she looked back to the plane, in time to see a small spout erupt where it had been. The rest of the plane was nowhere to be seen. As far as Jenny could tell only she and Jake had survived the crash.

She swam towards the island until her muscles were burning in protest and she couldn't move them with ease, by then she had reached a small rock face where she could hold onto a ledge while she waited for Jake to catch up. He was quick to follow her onto the ledge. Once they were both up and sitting on the wet rock they took pause to catch their breaths. The waves crashed against them as they sat in an inch of water breathing heavily. It was still cold and wet, but Jenny's muscles appreciated the small break from swimming.

She looked around, wondering if this was as far as they would be able to get. The island appeared to be a large rock wall. She looked up with fear, *would they have to climb to get to safety?* She wondered, knowing that eventually the tide would come in and the rock they were sitting on would end up underwater. She could see the salt stains halfway up the wall where the high tide would sit. They weren't safe yet.

"So, do you think we are the only ones?" Jenny asked after a minute, looking back to the slow bubbling crash site. She could only see it because it was breaking the waves as they crashed towards her.

Jake followed her gaze, "I hope not," he said quietly, watching the water with a sadness that consumed his whole body. He shook from the chill of the water, "I had a buddy on that plane."

"Me too." Jenny sucked in her breath, trying to hold back tears. They came anyway, warm and comforting, she heaved in a sob, "This sucks." She whispered over the sound of her own crying. Jake slid across the rock and put an arm over her shoulder, blocking her from the wind.

"If they are here, we will find them. Help will be on the way soon." He sounded like he was trying to convince himself more than Jenny, when she nodded, he smiled.

Jenny and Jake sat still on the rocks together, catching their breaths while they watched the last of the plane's tail end sink out of sight. They were soaked and the tropical breeze did little to warm them. Jenny moved closer, hoping to fend off some of the cold with body heat, she didn't know what to do next. Help should be on the way, but what about Grace and Ethan, what about Jerry? She was only there because Grace had asked her to come along, Grace had wanted to keep her safe. Where was Grace now? Who would keep her safe now?

RESCUE

Chung was fed up with all the time they were wasting bantering. He watched with determination out the small windows of the board room as a helicopter landed, sending a billow of leaves up into the air as it touched down. He stared at it with resolve while the lead agent continued his address, for Chung it went in one ear and out the other. Normally he was keen on protocol, his record was very clean and to the books. This time he cared little for his record and only for the safe return of Jenny.

He turned back to the lead agent as his address came to a close, the room was silent for a moment as they took in his parting words. From here it would be in King's hands.

"Move out." King called to the staring agents as he marched to the door, throwing it open with haste. Chung was right beside him, "You and I go first." He whispered to his partner, knowing it would take more than one trip of the helicopter to get them all out to Big Pine Key.

"Thanks." Chung hesitated for a moment, wanting to say more. Instead he bit his tongue and marched out to the helicopter, straight to the door while King selected the other agents that would be embarking with him on the first delivery to the Keys.

Finally they were on their way to Big Pine Key to ready a rescue team. The pinpoint location of the plane had yet to be established, the radio signal usually emitted by the planes black box had gone dark moments after the distress signal was emitted. The only thing they could assume was that it had landed somewhere in the Gulf of Mexico, and that left them with a large area to cover. Scout planes had already left to search for the wreckage. Chung sat in the helicopter fuming whilst the other agents talked tactics, he would go at this alone if they would let him have some of the equipment, but he knew there was no chance of that happening.

They landed slowly, scrambling out of the helicopter, heads down, as it took off to go pick up the next batch of agents. It was slow going, the Keys were not really equipped with accessible roadways out at the tip. They had a fleet of speedboats at their disposal, property of the coastguard, who would be escorting them on their rescue if the co-ordinates ever came in.

Chung checked his watch, time was passing even slower than he had imagined it to be. He felt as though the rescue were going in slow motion, he wanted to run, his patience was wearing thin.

"How much longer is this going to take?" Chung demanded of the first officer. Agent Nate Gromley stood stiffly waiting for the remainder of their team to arrive.

"We won't be leaving until all the pieces are in place, Chung." He seemed unfazed by the anger that was radiating from his comrade, believing that firm words could snap him out of his rage, "You need to clear your head. You'll be no good to anyone if you don't." He stared at Chung with insistence, planting his feet firmly.

"Can't we send the helicopter out to find the wreckage?" Chung stared him down, inches from his face, "They could be drowning out there for all we know. Stop being an idiot and use your head!" He shouted at the agent. Gromley stood his ground, watching over Chung's shoulder as King pulled him back to diffuse the tension.

Gromley looked at Chung sympathetically as he was pulled away, which was the last thing he wanted. Fuming, Chung stormed away across the docks to clear his head. Gromley turned to King, who was about to turn and follow his partner he placed a hand on King's shoulder, stopping him before he walked away.

"Look." He said standing stiffly. "I know this is frustrating, trust me, I wouldn't want to be in his shoes. But if he can't calm down, he can't come, I'm not putting the rest of the civilians in danger, Sir."

King chuckled, "You'd better hope his sister is alive out there, because if she's not, your job is going to be the least of your worries." He walked away slowly, watching as Gromley's face turned sour. He didn't care about formalities anymore, this was his family and he wasn't about to start taking lip from the Florida office.

King paced for a minute thinking the situation over as he watched Chung doing the same at the edge of the docks. Fury washed over him as he contemplated what his partner was going through, he knew how rough this situation was for him. Chung had far more at stake here. He righted his shoulders with resolve, he wasn't going to let it get to him.

King knew this was taking too long, he would give it an hour and then he was commandeering a boat. Come hell or high-water, they were getting their friends back alive. He rushed to tell Chung his plan, hoping it would calm him down before he got himself kicked out of the rescue team for his attitude.

Chung was pacing on the dock, watching the water with tired eyes, King got the feeling he was trying to see if he could find anything from there. He approached slowly, not wanting to incur the wrath of Chung with his flu and his sister's predicament. It was a thin line to walk to appease his partner.

He stopped a few feet behind him waiting for the opportune

moment to interrupt without causing Chung to go into a rage. Chung sensed his presence and stopped mid step to turn towards him.

"What now?" He demanded. King frowned, he had missed his cue.

"Look, I know this sucks..." King began, realizing this would be hard to explain to him in his state, "Jenny is one tough cookie, and if they don't get their heads outta their asses soon, we're taking off on our own." Chung's expression had changed from a scowl into a sly smile.

"I like your thinking." He waited for the rest with his arms crossed over his chest. King sized him up before he continued. He would have to appeal to Chung in a way that would not lose them their jobs, because at this point he looked like he was willing to kill anyone that stood in his way.

"So I figure, if we talk to one of the captains, we could get a boat out there in half an hour, tops." He stared at Chung for a moment longer, "But you have to let me do the talking..." That was the kicker, Chung reverted to his scowl, thinking it over for a minute. He knew King was a smooth talker and could probably make the arrangements without him, but knowing Jenny was out there had set him in motion and he was reluctant to accept any help. He nodded finally,

"Yeah, okay." He went back to his pacing while King walked off to find a captain who would be willing to listen.

***

Grace fell to her knees as the tail of the plane drifted out of sight. She felt suddenly helpless, Jenny had been sitting in the back of the plane and there was nothing she could do to fix that. Tears rolled silently down her cheeks as her mouth gaped open, it was her fault that Jenny was on that plane. She probably would have been safer at home. Grace pounded her fist into the sand with frustration, she had just gotten her best friend killed.

A hand landed on her shoulder, Jerry and Ethan were standing behind her looking pale at the sight they had just seen.

"She might have gotten out, Grace. She's a smart girl." It was Jerry trying to comfort her.

Grace stood slowly, gritting her teeth against the heart wrenching pain in her chest. She scanned the crowd looking for Jenny. Everyone was out of the water by now, at least everyone who had made it. She turned again, searching the small crowd, there was no sign of Jenny.

Others were watching the beach where the tail of the plane had disappeared in despair. There had been other passengers on board back there. Some of their families and friends were surely here on the beach, feeling the same as Grace was now. She searched the crowd for others feeling her grief, hopeful that they would be willing to go with her to search. She couldn't just leave Jenny out there floating away. If she had made it out she would be on the other side of the island. What if she was alone? Grace felt she was obligated to be sure that if Jenny was alive she was safe and if she wasn't... Grace wasn't ready to think of that possibility just yet.

Across the beach a man watched her silently, his face was contorted in sadness. He turned to the far beach where the plane had disappeared and then back to Grace, he began walking towards her silently. Grace looked away from him, embarrassed to be caught tearful. She turned back to Ethan and Jerry, resolved in her mind about what she was going to do next.

"I don't see her here." Grace pointed to the shivering crowd behind her.

"I know Grace." Ethan reached for her hand, still scanning the travelers behind her hoping to catch a glimpse of Jenny amongst them.

"If she isn't here, then she's with the tail of the plane." Grace pointed around the island where it had disappeared around the bend of the distant beach.

"Grace..." Ethan stared at her face, watching her teary eyes become steely with determination.

"I'm going to get her." Grace interrupted. "Chung would expect it of us, even if she is..." Grace paused, holding her breath. She started to sob again.

Her heaving breaths caught in her throat as she tried to hold herself together. She was aware that crying wouldn't help Jenny, but she couldn't stop the tears from flowing down her cheeks and her breath from catching in her throat. She wiped at her eyes with her sand covered hands, making it worse as her eyes then began to water from the sand she had wiped in them.

Ethan pulled her in, holding her tightly in his arms, "I'll see what we can do to get to her Grace, but for now, we should worry about staying with everyone else while we wait for help." He turned her shoulders towards the gathering crowd of survivors. There were about sixteen of them, wandering aimlessly across the beach, shivering in the breeze from the damp cold of the water that clung to their clothes.

A disheveled looking man walked towards them, his eyes were wide with fear. He smelled salty like the water, and the sand clung to his damp shoes as he trudged closer, watching them as he approached.

"Have you seen Jake?" He looked past them at the water, he held his hand up to his eyes, "He's about this tall, dark hair." His face fell as he searched the beach for a moment, lost in thought. "He was sitting at the back of the plane." He looked past them into the waves again, obviously hoping his friend would appear out of the deep.

Grace watched the man with despair, if his friend was also at the back and hadn't gotten to shore, then the chances of them finding Jenny were diminishing. She held in a fresh wave of tears, shaking her head as her eyes welled up again.

The man's face fell again, he struggled to speak, "I need to find him..." He whispered quietly, his eyes pleading with them.

Ethan shook his head, "I'm sorry, the tail of the plane went around the island, that way." He pointed away from the crowd. "I don't think we can catch up to it..." He looked to Grace knowing that his dismissal of this stranger's friend was a blow to her desire to find Jenny. He couldn't think of a way to make it better.

"That's what I thought." The man frowned deeply, then straightened himself up, his lip still quivering in protest, "Well then, I'm just gonna have to get to him." He began walking tentatively down the beach, Ethan raced after him before he could disappear.

Grace's eyes lit up with hope as she followed.

"Wait." She called after him, holding her hands out to him as he paused in the sand turning slowly.

"Let me come with you, we have a friend who was sitting in the back too." Ethan interrupted, watching Grace's face as the fire in her eyes burned to embers. He wasn't about to let her run off with a stranger on an island. "My name is Ethan." He held out a hand, stopping in the sand to catch his breath. The man stopped and took it in his.

"Bruce." He said in a hushed voice, shaking Ethan's hand firmly.

"Well Bruce, I think our best option is to go around to the other side and see if we can find the rest of the wreckage." Ethan said.

"That's what I was planning, good to have an extra set of eyes though." He nodded appreciatively at Ethan for the support.

Then with a flair, he turned to the rest of the crowd, "Anyone else want to go find the tail of the plane?" He called over their chatter.

The waiting crowd went silent, listening intently to the strange man who was bringing some order to their chaos. They watched Bruce with rapt attention.

"Anyone?" He called again once he had gained their attention.

Few faces looked up with determination, the crowd began murmuring as they thought the offer through. Soon, two came forward.

"We'll go. Our brother was sitting back there..." They yelled to Bruce as they walked to join the small group of travelers, they looked terrified at the choice they had just made.

Soon three others had come to join them, all with friends and family that had been in the back of the plane. They looked shaken and Ethan felt an overwhelming pity for them having to go through with this. Some of them didn't look like they would make the long trek, but who was he to deny them the chance to search for their friends? He nodded to each in turn, Grace approached from behind him and he turned to her.

Grace put her hand on Ethan's arm, "Are you sure we should all go?" She whispered to him, looking over their new companions. Ethan stared back at her with confusion.

"Grace, you aren't coming." He leaned in, pulling her close, watching Jerry from over her shoulder. He lowered his voice so only she could hear over the crashing waves, "Jerry can't make a trek like that, he'll need you here." He tried to break it to her easily. She bit her lip with frustration, pushing him back gently so she could give him a scolding look.

"So you think you'd be better in the wilderness than I would?" She crossed her arms and stared him down, "She's my friend Ethan and I need to find her." She pursed her lips waiting for him to cave in, hoping that he would commit to staying with Jerry so she could go to Jenny.

He looked into her eyes, unwavering, "Grace you are more important than anyone on this island." He whispered to her over the wind, "Be here when help comes and send them for us and Jenny." He took her hand "That is your job, to get us help."

"It could be your job. I would be better in the woods." Grace kept her tone sharp and soft, breathing the words into Ethan's ear as they debated who would venture on the quest across the island.

"Grace, you know better how to take care of Jerry. He doesn't have his meds. He needs *you*." Ethan took a step back, knowing that he had won the argument.

Grace looked at the ground, she knew he was right, she would be better here taking care of Jerry and signaling help. She hugged him and frowned over his shoulder at the strangers he was about to leave with, "Be safe then, I'll get started making a signal fire." She tried to sound calm, like this was just another adventure, but the wavering in her voice gave her away.

"I'll be back soon." He whispered.

"Thank you." Was all Grace could say, she knew he would go to the end of the earth for her happiness, she knew he would find Jenny for her.

Ethan held her tightly for a moment before turning back to the group that had gathered to find the back of the plane. It was time to make a plan.

They were already conversing when Ethan joined back in, talking about the best way to find the others, through the island or around on the beach. Ethan agreed with Bruce who was arguing that the forest would be faster, "Through is more direct, it will take less time, walking the whole way around the beach would take too much time."

"Staying on the beach would give us a better chance to see them from a distance." Argued one of the others.

It seemed like this discussion had been going on for a while, they were starting to look flustered, and Ethan worried that they were about to split up, which would do them no good in the long run. One of the groups was bound to get lost. They would be better if they stuck together, strength in numbers.

"No matter what direction we choose, we need to stick together, there is no sense in more of us getting lost." Ethan interrupted, drawing the attention of the small group. Reluctantly, they nodded in agreement.

"We should get started, the sooner the better. Is there anything we need to bring?" Asked the young man beside Bruce as he fidgeted his feet in the sand.

He looked like he was the leader of his small group, in search of a friend that had had the misfortune of arriving at the airport a moment too late to be seated with the others. His face was grim and he held fast to his belt, as though it usually held a utility of sorts that would have been removed for the flight at the security checkpoint if not sooner.

"I found a first aid kit." Bruce answered as he pulled out a small white box from his back pocket, it was unlikely to hold anything more than bandages and ibuprofen and was still dripping salt water.

"Let's head out then, through the woods?" Ethan spoke firmly, believing that it was the most direct route. He waited a minute for the others to respond, hoping they wouldn't get caught up in the forest versus beach argument again.

Slowly they nodded in agreement, turning to the woods to pinpoint their destination, then they would begin the trek.

Bruce nodded with gratitude towards Ethan for choosing the faster route and putting a stop to the debate as he tucked the first aid back into his pocket. "It's not much, but we might need it if someone is hurt." He muttered to Ethan.

He seemed determined that the passengers at the back had made it through the ordeal unscathed. Ethan worried that he was wrong, but he couldn't bring himself to debate the state of the passengers from the rear of the plane. Whatever had happened to them, Jenny was among them.

Of the thirty some odd people on the flight less than twenty had washed ashore so far, the odds were not looking so good to him. He was doing this for Grace, recovering Jenny's body so she could rest in peace knowing her friend wasn't still floating around out there. He didn't know how they were going to break this to Chung. He wondered if he already knew the plane had gone down, or if they even knew that they were out here. Ethan expected they were waiting for them in Florida, ready to escort the group to a safe house, meeting them at the airport as a surprise. It seemed this time the surprise was on them.

How long would it take for word to get out that their plane had crashed? How long until King and Chung were on route to rescue them? Ethan sighed heavily at the thought that he needed to be saved, again. If there were a way to get them off of this island and into the safe house on his steam, he would have done it by now. It seemed he was destined to wait for assistance, yet again. This time he was going to do as much as he could to get them through this unscathed and that meant finding Jenny.

With a small frown, he righted his shoulders and walked forward with the others across the beach. Wet shoes squishing against his waterlogged socks as he stepped, rubbing sand against his ankles as it collected on his damp skin.

It was going to be a long walk.

RESTLESS

Chung paced by the boats waiting for the signal to leave, his impatience had reached its peak.

The plane's transponder had been located off the coast and they were soon to be heading out to retrieve it. Supplies were being loaded into the boats and helicopters were in the air trying to use the location of the black box to find the wreckage.

Chung was watching the choppers from the dock while more crew passed him by with crates of medical supplies. His hands trembled as he watched the choppers circling in the distance, barely visible near the horizon.

Chung listened to the chatter of the crew while he watched, eavesdropping for information that could tell him what to expect. He steeled himself for the worst as he heard a stream of conversation between two crew members carrying a crate to one of the boats.

"They think the pilots are dead." Said the first as he grunted under the weight of the crate.

"If that's true than I doubt the passengers made it." Said the second.

Chung tensed as they moved out of earshot, this was worse than he had thought.

They didn't have any way of knowing if there were any survivors yet, the choppers were circling the bay in search of a more pinpoint direction for them to head in. It was suspiciously silent in the water, he listened to the waves crashing against the hull of the boat nearest him. The day was growing late, he could feel the cool evening breeze blowing through his opened jacket.

Wherever Jenny and the others were, he hoped they were safe. They couldn't have stayed afloat for this long, he hoped they had found an inflatable boat or something. He wracked his head for the safety procedures airplanes used, forgetting the safety instructions from the beginning of every flight he had ever taken. It was always in one ear and out the other, next time he would pay attention.

King walked up behind him, stomping his feet on the creaking dock to announce his presence. He held in his hand a bag of sandwiches and two cold coffees, a small offering for his flustered partner to appease his impatience.

"How are you?" King asked staring out at the water, it was part of their man code to never make eye contact when something serious was happening and what had happened to Jenny and the others was very serious. Chung respected the privacy King had allowed him without removing him from the rescue team like he probably should have. Taking one of the coffee cups from King's outstretched hand, he breathed it in deeply, taking a mouthful before answering.

"I just want to get this over with." He took another sip, relieved as the caffeine surged through him, cold and calming. "It's been too long, it's not going to be good." The realization washed over him as he spoke the words aloud. The realization that they were probably stalling because it was a recovery more than a rescue they were going in for. No one had told him yet, but he had heard them talking, he suspected they were all dead.

Quietly he stood watching the water lapping against the dock as he let the coffee work its way through his system, waking him back up again. He felt dead inside, waiting for what he could only assume would be bad news. He couldn't decide which would be worse, hearing the news from afar, or being in the thick of it. He wanted to walk off of the case and head back to Washington, somehow his heart wouldn't let him.

"Makes you wonder...what's taking them so long?" Chung muttered under his breath as he took another swig of his coffee. He turned to King with a seriousness that had rarely occurred between the two partners.

King was taken back at the gesture, "I wish I could tell you..." Were the only words he could think to speak.

"Does that mean you know something?" Chung was stern, his voice quivering.

"Not any more than you." King stared off at the fleet of boats awaiting departure. After a moment of contemplation Chung turned to join his stare.

"Good." He whispered.

***

"Are you ready?" Jenny called to Jake over the rush of the rising tide.

They had rested long enough, the threat of the rising water pushed them to continue their trek, taking them up the side of the rock face. They had been staring at it for nearly ten minutes as the tide had grown, washing water up to their knees. It was now or never if they hoped to reach the top before the water consumed them.

"After the next wave." Jake called, watching as a large tumbling wall of water made its way towards them. He didn't want to risk being tossed off the wall once they started their climb. They would have less than a minute after the crash before the next one came in, they needed to move quickly.

"Now!" He called a moment later as the crash subsided enough for them to pull themselves onto the rocks above their heads.

Jenny reached for the rocks quickly, watching above her at the places she had observed to be decent footholds while she had waited at the bottom. Her arms and legs still ached from the swim to the island. The saltwater clung to her as she fought through the first wave, crashing her against the wall. She kept her hold as Jake tumbled back down below her onto the outcropping.

"Hurry up!" She called down encouragingly as he began to climb again.

Soon he was at the same height, searching for the next place to grasp on the slippery wall.

Jenny quickly realized how difficult climbing a cliff really was. From below it had looked like a walk in the park, a quick trip up to the island proper. Now that she was halfway there with the crashing waves taunting her below and the glaring sun catching her eyes, she wasn't sure what she had gotten herself into. Failing was no longer an option, she needed to be able to get to help for her friends. If she even slipped a little there was a sharp outcropping of waterlogged rocks waiting to catch her below. The gravity of the situation really sunk in when she reached for her next hand hold and a large chunk of rock dislodged itself from the wall, cracking down on her head and slicing her hand in the process. She held steady for a moment, breathing deeply as she caught herself.

"You alright over there?" Called Jake from somewhere on her left, she listened as the rock tumbled, crashing silently into the angry water below.

Jenny couldn't talk, she was suddenly paralyzed with fear, stuck on a rock face with nowhere to go but up. With each inch she made upwards, it was one more inch she knew she could fall into the depths below. She grasped at the wall in a panic, Jake called to her again.

"Jenny? Are you alright?" The words sounded muted as they passed through her ears. She pressed her face against the cold rock wanting to stay there forever.

"Jenny." Jake called again, "You need to keep moving."

The day had passed quickly for Jenny and Jake as they tried to reach the top of the slippery rock face before the tide grew higher. It pressed at their heels forcing them to move faster despite their fatigue. They had dried off from their initial dip in the cold waters below, but the sprinkling of saltwater from the crashing waves rising from the base of the rock face kept them damp and shivering and the rocks slippery and dangerous.

"We're almost at the top." Jake called back over his shoulder, reaching for another rock to pull himself up onto. He yelped as his hand fell back at his side, failing to catch a proper grip on the rock above him. As his heart shuttered in his chest, he looked down at the water crashing at the wall, slowly reaching for Jenny's feet as he made his way up the wall behind her. Swinging back towards the wall, he set his sight upwards and onward, again reaching for the rocks above. This time he tested his grip with more caution before letting his foot free of the rock outcropping below for another foothold.

Beside him Jenny was catching up, she moved with reflexes that seemed abnormally calculated, as though climbing a perilous rock wall were as normal to her as a stroll in the park. He watched with awe as she passed him, reaching for the top of the cliff face with fatigued ease.

"Come on, don't quit now." Jenny called, encouraging her seatmate to continue the climb. He was the only one she had now, if he gave up then she was doomed to wander the woods alone. She pulled herself up and over the edge, flat onto her stomach at the top of the cliff, wiping the sting of saltwater from her eyes so she could see.

When she turned to look down, she realized how far they had come. Even with the tide rising, it was a long way to the bottom. "Just a little more." She called to Jake as he made the final climb to join her at the top.

She knelt down and reached for his hand, giving him a tug to help him over the top. He crawled away from the edge, breathing heavily. She followed, collapsing in a heap when she thought she was far enough away to avoid the risk of falling. Her muscles ached, they burned from the strain of the swim combined with the exertion of the climb. She couldn't feel her shoulders, but suspected the pain would reach her in a day or so when she regained the feeling back. Together, they lay in a heap watching as the horizon grew dark before them.

"We made it." Jake gasped through panting breaths.

"Thanks," Jenny whispered after her racing heart and aching lungs had had time to recover slightly. "I couldn't have done it without you."

"Any time," Jake smirked through a stitch in his side, "That was crazy..." He breathed slowly as he stood to look over the cliff. He watched the gentle waves, leaving no sign of the turmoil they had just escaped from. It was as though the water had swallowed the plane whole, leaving nothing behind but the two survivors overlooking from the tall cliff of the island.

"There's nothing left..." He breathed in awe.

She sat beside him, watching in the dying light as the waves crashed towards the island, leaving no trace of the plane they had come from. They were truly alone.

"I can't believe it," she whispered, "how will they find us now?"

She looked up into Jake's staring eyes.

"I don't know."

Jenny nodded in agreement, sadly. The whole thing seemed to play back in her head like a movie she had watched from a distance, she couldn't believe that it was all real. The plane crash, the swim, the climb up the rocks. She would never have imagined in a thousand years that she would end up here.

"Now what?" Jenny was growing quieter, her body began to shake from the cold and the aches in her muscles became permanent as the numbness washed slowly away.

"I don't know..." Jake trailed off, lost in thought as he recounted the events that had transpired that day, wistfully playing out a scenario where his friend had made it out alive; and dreading telling the bride otherwise.

The light was fading fast and Jenny knew she had exhausted all of her energy getting safely onto the island, "I don't suppose we could miraculously find wood to start a fire?" She asked with worry as darkness fell across them.

Jake turned to look at the island around them, seeing only shadows and silhouettes in the dim light, "Probably not."

"Do you think the island is safe?" Jenny asked next, listening for the howl of a wolf or the scurry of a creature in the distance.

"I suppose we'll just have to find out." Jake said, taking a step closer to Jenny.

Jenny went silent beside him, wondering how long it would take for help to find them and how the others had fared at the front of the plane. She still wanted to believe that they had made it, though she feared that they had not.

She steeled herself against the emotions coursing through her, focusing now on her survival so she could tell their story. She hadn't had time while they were climbing the rocks to process the plane crash. It felt like a thing of the past, the memories of that morning were fuzzy in her mind as though she hadn't really been there at all. She was sure it was just survivors guilt, preventing her from seeing the accident clearly, blocking it from her mind to save her from the pain and the guilt.

She regretted that the others had been at the front of the plane, maybe if they had all been seated together they wouldn't be in this situation now, or maybe she wouldn't have made it either. Jenny watched the darkness approaching with reverence. She would need to signal for help eventually, to let the inevitable rescue team know that they were here and had made it. But for now she only wanted to be dry and warm while she mourned for her friends.

INVESTIGATION

Boats were pulling away from the dock with astounding speed, the roaring engines cut through the radio calls. A crowd had gathered around the dock, watching the rescue team, pushing and prying for a good view.

News casters and radio stations waited for their two minutes of air time as they tried vigorously to cover the unexpected plane wreckage for their viewers. The excitement dripped off of them as they enthusiastically breathed in the sorrow and the loss.

Chung watched them with stoic eyes, disappointed in the human race for its need of violence. His sister waited in peril or perhaps was already dead and all they wanted was their story. Not one of them offered a helping hand, instead they clamored across the dock blocking the passage of rescue crews, impeding their ability to save those that may have survived. He hissed in their direction as they became specks on the horizon, how much better the world would be without them.

The wreckage had been found, at least half of it. King was afraid to tell Chung that the tail end had been separated. It had drifted away in a current before the black box had been found and the front of the wreckage discovered. King had read through the passenger manifesto several times since then, hoping he was misreading it. He reached for his vest pocket to be sure it was still tucked safely away from the weather and Chung's prying eyes.

The manifesto showed that Jenny had had a seat in the back. King flashed a fleeting glance at his partner as the boat shook atop a wave. She was still out there somewhere with any luck. Maybe she had even used her charm to get her seat switched once they were on board, he could always hope.

In the back of his mind he knew this salvage mission would not find her though. He wished he had better news to share with Chung to balance out the inevitable recoil of the current initiative. Instead he bit his tongue, waiting for the news to pass to Chung through the usual channels, wondering what he could say to ease the blow.

Waves crashed against the hull, spraying salty water into King's eyes while the boats sped in formation towards the site. Overhead the whirring engine of a helicopter churned, stirring up more waves as it ushered them in. He held his breath and the rail, the boat began to slow. He braced himself for the scene he expected to find before them. Chung looked tense, peering off the side of the boat desperately searching the still empty waters for a sign of life, for a sign of Jenny.

The salty water clung to Chung's face, churning his stomach as it infiltrated his mouth and nostrils. He wiped the salt from his forehead where it clung, making his skin stiff. Staring forward he bit his lip against the pain in his chest. He wanted to believe he would see his sister again.

The helicopters overhead were retreating, he watched with frustration when they stirred up the already vicious water below. How would the survivors have fared in the white-capped waters? He watched their approach, knowing with the choppers' departure that they were closing in on the site. He stared ahead, hoping for a sign of movement.

More than once he was elated at the thought that he had seen a hand waving, his heart would drop when he realized he was staring at a piece of debris caught on a swell of water.

The boats cut their speed when they began to reach debris, floating luggage and clothing were strewn across the water. It had been washed out by the current and had spread as far as the eye could see ahead of them. It looked like a floating wasteland, eerily silent and void of life.

King sucked in a sharp breath steeling himself in the event that they found bodies, the silence of the waters told him this place held no life. The captain slowed to a halt, reaching overboard with a hook to pull debris away. He pointed to the side of the boat, turning a stern face towards the waiting agents.

"More hooks over there, call if you find a body." The starkness of his words caught the attention of Chung, who took a moment to look up from the waters lapping lullaby. Quickly he had reached for a hook and crossed the deck to search on the opposite side.

King's face went white, "What about the rest of the plane?" He looked out to the diminishing shadow of the dilapidated aircraft, still floating with a deflated slide hung out the front doors, barely visible in the distance.

"Still looking, probably sunk already." He coughed while he pulled in a bag from the water. The plane bubbled in the distance, lowering into the water. From one of the other boats two divers dipped below the waves, making their way cautiously towards the wreckage in search of survivors inside. King watched them in the shivering waves, passing through the scattering of overhead baggage as they worked their way to the wreckage. He reached over the side of the boat for a hook to aid the crew with the removal of debris. A purse floated by, scattering its female contents across a wave as it toppled. King hooked it in, searching it for a piece of identification, wondering if it could be Grace's or Jenny's. An unfamiliar name dotted the license in the dripping wallet. He let out a breath, not realizing he had been holding it in. Slowly he set the purse aside; if she had made it she might want it back, he reasoned.

Night was falling quickly, the setting sun blared across the horizon. King pulled out a set of sunglasses to stop the glare. Clouds passed overhead taking with them the last of the dying rays. As dusk fell the radios went wild with conversation from one boat to another. The captain recoiled from the side of the boat to take his turn on the speaker. Soon the crew was bustling around the deck opening black cases that had been brought aboard; generators for the large spotlight they had uncovered in the center of the vessel.

With a bright flash across the water, the spotlights began to glow across the scene. In the new light Chung looked across the water, hoping to see flailing arms, or hear pleas from passengers alive in the water. It was eerily silent over the beeping of the Doppler and the crash of the waves. They worked in silence, pulling in luggage as they searched for bodies.

Most of the floating debris was overhead baggage that had come loose, probably in the crash itself. Purses and bags were pulled aboard to identify the passengers. When all else failed they had the manifesto, but loved ones would appreciate the proof if they couldn't recover the bodies.

As they kept working it was beginning to look like they wouldn't, no bodies floated amongst the debris that Chung had sifted through, though air masks glowed in the water, proof that life had once been here. He frowned, there should be some bodies somewhere. He was caught between grief and elation that perhaps there was still a slim chance that Jenny and the others were out there, floating lazily in a big yellow dingy. He scanned the horizon against the glare of the lights, hopeful of finding it. But beyond the lights, all was lost in the dark of night.

After several hours of searching they had pulled in a large portion of the luggage. The boat was teemed with damp bags and debris when the captain pulled in his hook.

"Time to take it to forensics, we'll come back after they've unloaded." King looked at him with remorse. They were heading back to the dock, refueling and starting over. No bodies had turned up yet, they hadn't even reached the plane. The bodies were probably still inside, buckled in for safety.

DARKNESS

Grace and Jerry had been scouring the tree line for most of the afternoon, making small piles of sticks and broken twigs to bring down to the beach for the signal fire. It was harder work than she had anticipated. Grace kept glancing over her shoulder at Jerry, making sure he wasn't working himself too hard. The thick brush of the woods kept them from wandering in too far, she tried to keep the crowd on the beach in view just in case. It wouldn't be good if she and Jerry got lost, especially as dusk made way to darkness. The dim light of the stars kept her moving through the late evening hours, but as the darkness grew more absolute, she had to call it.

"Jerry, I think we've done enough." She placed a hand on his shoulder, taking the branches from his arms into her own as she stooped to recover the rest that they had managed to find.

"I know, it's getting too dark out here for my old eyes." He stopped as his chuckle turned into a deep cough. Grace could hear his chest rattling in protest as he breathed heavily. He wasn't doing very well, she needed to keep him safe.

Grace led the way when she and Jerry made their trip back to the beach, carrying what little they had found to add it to the pile. The slick sand had become cold after the sun had disappeared for the evening, the chill of the island became absolute. A cool breeze trickled through as they reached the exposure of the beach, Grace saw Jerry shivering as the rattling of his breathing grew louder. She passed him a wary glance, stepping between him and the wind, hoping that it would be enough to prevent his cold from growing worse. They needed fire, not only to attract help, but for warmth as well.

The beach had come alive shortly after Ethan's departure. One man had taken charge and ordered, in the politest way possible, that the waiting crowd begin their search for enough wood to start a signal fire. He had argued that they would also need it for warmth when the evening breeze began to grow cold, he had been right. The night air was enough to chill them to the bones.

Like worker ants they had scattered in groups searching far and wide for logs and other dry brush. The island had been damp when they arrived, a passing storm just missing their arrival on its own departure.

In the dark, the small motley group had gathered around the pile of wood they had managed to scour from within the woods. Without the light they would have no chance of starting their fire tonight, instead they stood, staring at the wood wishing for a miracle.

"This is the last of it." Grace announced, knowing that she and Jerry were the last ones to emerge from the woods that evening. She dropped her small pile onto the rest looking at it with a frown.

The pile was sparse and composed mostly of broken twigs and wet driftwood. Grace frowned at it, knowing it would be hard to light with all the damp wood that had been tossed in. If they did get it going it would create a lot of smoke, though it would be seen from a distance in the dark.

"Thanks." One of the men around the pile commented, leaning in to start piling the wood properly for the start of a fire. Grace leaned down to help, creating a small triangle shaped pile with the smaller leaves and mulch set in the center.

They placed it just outside of the forests edge, knowing that once they got the fire started it would need to be seen. The beach didn't provide them any cover from the elements, so they had tried their best to resolve the issue of a cold night by keeping the pile close to the edge where they could duck and cover if a storm blew in. Grace looked up at the twinkling stars, she could tell by the breeze that something was blowing in. Soon the sky would be a more profound black. She shivered in the whipping wind, hoping it would hold off until the fire was set.

Now there was just the matter of lighting the fire, they had found matches among the floating wreckage, but they were useless now that they had been exposed to the water. Grace had found three lighters, but they were suffering from the same demise, unable to produce even a spark in their dampness. She had asked someone to try and get them dry while she had continued to look for wood.

That had been earlier in the day she hoped that by now they had them working, but she couldn't remember who had been given the task of drying them. They were going to need the fire soon, especially if the cool wind kept up.

Jerry was weary from the day that he had endured, he was faint from the sun beating off of his uncovered head for most of the day. His brain was pounding in his skull, he knew he was dehydrated and that saltwater wasn't drinkable. He wasn't sure how he could help the small group of survivors, but rather than hinder their efforts, he sat at the edge of the forest out of the way thinking. His breath caught in his throat again, he heaved, coughing violently. He could hear his chest rattling as he breathed and wished he had managed to keep some of his medications with him during the departure.

He had recognized some of the landmarks out of the windows on the way down, although they didn't make much sense to him. They had been flying to Miami, how had they overshot it by that much? Even a circling plane would have no reason to be flying over the Florida Keys. He scrunched his nose, wincing at the burning as his skin bunched. He was sunburned already. He watched the crowd, searching for that flight attendant, maybe she would know why they were this far off of their flight path. He hadn't seen her since they arrived, he tried to remember the name on her badge and couldn't. He felt awful, she probably hadn't made it, ushering out the passengers first, it was her job and here he couldn't even remember her name to thank her.

He stood stiffly, his joints pained him more than he had ever thought they could. He walked to the edge of the water, watching as the waves rolled darkly over debris that had scattered through the water. The tide began rolling back in after a day at bay, it brought with it memories of the plane crash, mementos of those that hadn't made it to land.

Bodies were washing onto the beach.

Grace came up behind him, pulling him from the scene, "We found a lighter that works. The fire is getting going, come and warm up Jer." She took his hand and tugged him from the wet sand up the beach to sit with the others. As he walked with her, she looked back seeing what was coming ashore behind them. She pulled him faster, "I'll take care of that in a moment Jerry, it'll be alright." But they both knew it never would.

***

Ethan had followed Bruce as far as they could manage in the dwindling light, they had nothing with them but the small safety kit and it would not suffice for the food and water that they desperately needed. Ethan ached with every step he took and with every pause his muscles burned in protest, he couldn't win.

"I think we should stop for a while and rest," Ethan slowed, waiting for the others to catch up to him in the brush, "we can't see where we are going, and we're probably going to end up walking in circles if we keep going."

Ethan was panting from the tiresome walk through the brush and undergrowth of the forest. It had not been an easy trek for the lot of them. He had expected a clear path that would take them to their destination, instead they found themselves wandering through thick brush and dense trees weaving their way towards a destination that they had lost in the thick forest.

The others had reached the small clearing where he and Bruce waited. Heaving silently they lowered themselves to the ground, falling heavily in their haste to reserve what little energy they had left.

"How much farther do you think it is?" One of them asked after a moment.

"Shouldn't be far from here," Bruce replied, trying to look through the forest ahead of them for a sign of a beach. "If we rest for a little, it should be a quick trip, can't see anything now though." He shook his head looking to the ground. "Right then."

Bruce took a stick off of the forest ground and pegged it into the damp earth, "That'll mark the way when we *can* see again." He sat himself down panting from the exertion of the trip. Here there were no paths, no way to see out to know where they were, or if they were heading the right way. They had simply put their destination ahead of them on the beach and walked forward hoping to keep going in a straight line as they stumbled through the wild forest.

Bruce suspected that they had already walked through poison ivy and oak, the forest was so dense that is was almost a certainty that they would be itching their way back to the beach, if they ever found the others.

Now in the dark of the night, Bruce was regretting their decision to cross inland. Although it may have taken longer to reach the other side where the tail end had floated off to from the beach, at least they would have had the stars to guide them through the night, now he doubted they would get there in time. If Jake needed help, he would have needed it before Bruce could get to him and there was no guarantee that the tail end of the plane had not just carried on in a current. It could be long gone before they ever reached the other side of the island.

Nodding his head forward, Bruce fell asleep sitting against a tree. Worried lines creased his face in the dark. His mind drifted to old memories of his lost friend, the guilt was only washed away when his exhaustion took over sending him into a fitful sleep.

Ethan, as exhausted as he was, couldn't shut down. His mind was spinning and he had taken to pacing quietly on the outskirts of the small clearing they had chosen for camp. It didn't help that he kept tripping over the same tree roots over and over, resetting his jumbled thoughts as he fumbled for his footing over again. His mind was racing, should he really have left Grace and Jerry on the beach? When would help come? Had it come already? Had he been left behind? And though he didn't want to think about it, his mind wandered onto the possibility that Jenny could be dead and he may be unable to get to her.

The others were whispering in the night, quieter than the rustling of the trees. He wondered what they were talking about. Suddenly he was absolutely aware that he didn't know any of them. Even if he could sleep, he didn't feel comfortable laying down in their presence. He couldn't risk trusting the wrong person and given the circumstances surrounding their departure to Florida, even telling them too much about who he was could be dangerous. He was on his way to a safe house, fake names and ID's awaited him. He kicked himself for even telling them his real name back at the beach.

Ethan could hear Bruce snoring softly, he too, was alone in the woods. His only companion lost in the wreckage, Ethan wanted to believe that he could trust that man. The sincerity in his pleading eyes back at the beach had struck a chord with him. Knowing that Bruce had drifted off made Ethan's mind up for him, he would stand guard while the others slept. Anything could be on this island, wild animals, snakes and what if help came? They could be abandoned in the woods if they didn't hear the calls. He stood silently against a tree, thinking as he listened to the whispering chatter across the clearing become silent, knowing that the others had also fallen asleep. Now he was alone in the woods.

At first it seemed a relief, he could think through the events of the day and get all of his worries laid out on the table. The silence of his companions soon began to take its toll on him. Every breeze crackling a leaf, or shuffle of a foot in their troubled sleep, set his heart beating. The darkness under the canopy of the trees was almost absolute.

Ethan began pacing again, slowly, taking each step with caution and purpose. He kept the tree he had been leaning on within his arm's reach for safety. His eyes were growing heavy as he reached the peak of the night. His head nodded forward on him several times, jolting him awake as he realized that sleep was taking over.

The night was black, Ethan tried to stare through the upper foliage to see the stars. It was too dark and dim, the cloud cover left them under the cloak of night. Still he stared upwards, trying to clear his mind of the events that had led him into this predicament. Never in a thousand years would he have believed it if someone had warned him that he would become lost on a desolate island, never. The woods were silent, save the rustling of the leaves in the trees. It was eerie and unnatural, he listened harder, knowing that there had to be something alive out in the brush. A sudden chill swept up his spine as he thought of the creatures that could be watching them from the darkness. He took another slow quiet step, listening still as he paced the clearing, suddenly curious.

He stopped pacing abruptly, standing with his back to the tree, he could hear something in the woods. Fear crept through him as he separated the sound of the wind tousled leaves and the crinkling of a predator walking on the fallen leaves. It started in the distance, a whispering of leaves when the wind wasn't blowing. Soon it began to grow louder, still faint to the untrained ear. Ethan stood as still as his aching muscles would allow, hoping that whatever it was it wouldn't sense him and the others in the thick forest.

Bruce snored loudly, shifting in his restless sleep. Ethan caught his breath waiting for the rustling in the clearing to subside, he held his ear towards the forest, trying to catch the faint sound of crinkling leaves as something approached. It took him a moment to pick it up again and as he had feared, it was growing closer.

He thought about waking the others to warn them, but shook the thought off quickly. It could be a rabbit, or a skunk. He had no way of knowing if it was even a danger and the commotion of alerting the others would only draw it in if it was a predator. So he stood still, praying that it changed course as he listened for more movement.

Behind him there came a crackling in the woods, it was so quiet he couldn't be sure he had really heard it and then it came again, closer and he was more sure that he had heard something approaching. He paused to listen, tuning his ears to perceive what his eyes could not. Something was approaching slowly and stealthily, it breathed deeply as it passed inches from his face. He held his breath, fearful of a wild beast. Given the heftiness of the footfalls and the sound of its breaths he could be sure it was no small raccoon. Ethan held fast, still as he could muster, he found himself holding his breath to complete his desired invisibility. Across the clearing it was a black kind of dark and Ethan could not tell if the others had been alerted of the presence among them. He was too vulnerable to warn them as the footsteps paced back towards him, passing closer again. He felt a hot breath at his neck as the rustling breathed by him, again moving towards the clearing.

Ethan froze, as far as he knew the rest of the group had fallen asleep and he was the only one awake in the woods. He listened intently, his body held stiff against the tree behind him. Closing his eyes he focused on the sounds coming from across the clearing. Within a moment he had picked out the restful breaths of the others who had settled in for a short rest, Bruce's wheezing soft snore was coming from beside him at the base of the next tree. Yet the dripping splashes of water, the rustling of fabric and a sloshing container were tracing the area, coming from an unknown body. There came a sudden pop as a torch lit, followed by a flash of light. Beside him footsteps sounded loud and hurried, brushing past him. It nearly knocked him from his feet. He righted himself turning to the light in the woods. Before him a blaze was growing, it began to move through the woods. Soon a screeching sound accompanied the waving, wandering fire.

It was a person.

Ethan raced forward, caught in the rush of the others waking to the horrible screeching. One of the others had been set on fire. Pieces of fire dropped off as his clothing began to deteriorate. The fire was trying to spread across the damp leaves and failing. Above, the trees began to let through a sprinkling of rain that had begun above them and Ethan was hopeful for a moment that they would be able to put the fire out. The small group that had been slumbering in the brush had begun chaotically racing around the clearing throwing sticks, twigs and even articles of their own clothing at the flaming man to try and stifle the fire.

Across the small clearing Bruce jumped to his feet his face glowed in the flickering fire, "What the hell is happening? how is he on fire?" His eyes were wide in the glow of the flame and his voice wavered with fear.

Ethan had turned away from the spectacle, trying to locate the source of the footfalls that had raced past him. He avoided the stares of the others with him, their eyes wide and reflecting the dancing flames. It was too horrible a horror to behold. The air was thick with a stench that he could not place, something he never wanted to smell again. It could only be described as death. He tried to use the dwindling light behind him to see further into the woods, after whatever had raced off past him. He hoped to glimpse a flash of a shadow, or movement somewhere nearby. The pattering of light rain impeded his goal, the forest was alive with dropping water and the dim lights of the fire hadn't widened his search area by much. Finally he turned back to the others.

Bruce hovered near the screaming victim, unsure how to help him as his cries slowly died out. The companion that had come with him looked on in anguish, paralyzed with guilt and stricken with horror at what had become of his friend after surviving the initial crash of the plane. Behind him the other three huddled together, whispering. Ethan watched them with concern, not quite trusting that one of them hadn't caused the fire and circled back. Had they been awake? Had they done this? They were wide eyed, but he wasn't sure he believed them. He wasn't sure he could trust any of them.

"We shouldn't have come." He whispered almost too loud in the quiet woods as the screaming subsided. Finally the body fell to the forest floor, smoldering and smoking against the damp leaves. It was obvious he was dead.

They watched as a spark took, flashing across the ground in a trail like a sparkler across the ever dampening foliage. Ethan backed away from the moving fire, cautious of its destination. Soon it began to wind around the trees, twisting with a mind of its own, not natural to the movement of a flame, it began to spell. After a moment it was finished, *"soon"* scrolled across the forest floor for just an instant. The others looked on with horror and confusion.

Ethan's heart beat against his chest in an unnatural fashion, he held his hand to his heart to stop it while he watched the word die out on the forest floor. The world began to spin under his feet, he reached for the tree behind him to steady his lurching body. Fear crept through every inch of him as he watched the others in their shadowy movements, their voices were drowned out by the ringing in his ears.

Ethan no longer suspected they had anything to do with the fire, the words hissed as the storm overhead sent droplets of water through the trees, slowly killing the smoldering ash as they hit the ground. With each drop, the word became less visible, the hissing water smoked upwards. They all stood staring until the letters had fully vanished and the trickle of rain had become a torrent.

Ethan glanced up to see their faces in the dark watching their silhouettes through the trickle of rain. They looked confused at the spectacle before them, but to Ethan it was all too familiar.

DISTURBED

Jenny awoke with a start, she didn't remember falling asleep against Jake at the top of the cliff. The air was cold and dark. A dampness clung in the breeze as a light trickle of rain began to fall, giving her a chill that surely must have awoken her. She shifted to cover her exposed arm from the cold that was beginning to creep through her, she turned towards Jake to see if it had woken him too.

He sat back stiffly. Stretching slowly, he glanced to the sky, "Looks like rain," he whispered groggily, "gonna make it hard to start a signal fire." He added quietly, brushing the dampness from his pants. He stared at Jenny in the darkness.

"We should probably find some shelter from the rain." She suggested. She could hear the patter of droplets hitting the rocks now. The light mist was giving way to droplets as the storm grew stronger, a gust of wind brushed past them as though it were making a point.

A screeching sound erupted from behind them quite suddenly, they both turned to stare towards the dark woods. It was eerie noise, bone chilling and frightening all at once.

"What *is* that?" Jenny whispered, reaching for Jake in the dark.

He placed his hand on hers, "I have no idea."

The sound that had broken through the silent night was atrocious, it sounded like the wailing cry of a banshee. The piercing shriek rung in Jenny's ears as it echoed across the otherwise quiet island.

"What is that?" Jenny asked again with concern. She had never heard of an animal making noises like that, it almost sounded as though it were in pain.

"I don't know." Jake repeated slowly, "it doesn't sound like any animal I have ever heard before..." Jake breathed quietly, his eyes wide with fear. He had turned himself on the damp ground to face the still forest. The cry echoed louder.

"Then what could it be?" Jenny whispered, suddenly worried that she hadn't considered if the island was inhabited by some sort of wild beast.

Jake shook his head slowly, shaking the dampness from his hair as he went, "It sounds like a human...." he paused as the sound grew hoarser and quieter in the distance, "a human screaming in agony." His face contorted in response to the noise like he could almost feel the pain of the screamer, it was unsettling.

"Oh..." Jenny's face went white in the dark of the night when she considered what could have happened to make a person scream like that. There was no rustling or growling to accompany the sound, just the sheer agony of the voice in the woods, piercing through the night air.

"That means there are others out there," Jake commented with a stiff shrug after the sound lessened. He was wary of searching for the source, especially in the dead of night. His neck ached from straining to see the woods. If someone were out there in that much pain he would hate to fall into the same peril wandering into the black woods to find them. "We should wait and find them in the morning....if help hasn't already come by then." He hoped that by morning help would have arrived and then *they* could find the source of the wailing in the woods.

Jenny turned her neck to look up at him, "That's a good idea." She sat up fully, stretching away from Jake embarrassed, "Sorry I fell asleep on you, I didn't know I was so tired." She smiled awkwardly in the dark.

"It's okay, you kept me warm." Jake smiled back as the clouds above them opened up with a loud crackle. Rain began to pelt down on them, drenching them in an instant. Jenny stood, scanning the dark outcropping for some shelter with her limited range of vision. Soon the water was coming down in sheets, threatening to push them back over the edge of the cliff face as it quickly became a torrent of slippery waves around them.

"Really?" Jenny called out over the cliff to the sky, upset that Mother Nature was pelting her after the day she had just had.

Jake called to her as the water made the rocks slippery beneath her feet, "We should move into the woods for shelter." He called over the pattering.

"What if something is out there?" She called back, afraid of encountering the cause of the screaming that was still etched in her mind.

"We'll find somewhere safe." Jake promised.

She nodded. Realizing that he probably couldn't see her, she finally called back to him, "Okay, I'm coming."

With one fleeting glance back at the cliff and the black waters beyond, Jenny turned to the woods. Instantly her mind was filled with regrets. What if their retreat into the woods left the rescue team unable to find them? What had happened to the others? What if they were lost forever? With tears in her eyes, she walked forward into the dark, praying it would be over soon.

The rocks were slippery under her feet. She had to take small steps until she reached dirt that would provide her with better traction. The rain was coming down in sheets, making puddles of muck that coursed over her already ruined shoes. She cursed herself for wearing such impractical footwear on the plane, her flats slipped against the muck and after a few tumbles Jake slowed to help her.

"Here hold my arm." He said softly, walking back beside her.

"Thanks." Jenny was embarrassed, but she held his arm. He walked with her slowly towards the woods. Soaking wet and covered in mud, she felt hopeless.

"Hang on." Jake stopped beside Jenny, letting go of her arm for a moment, "Might as well rinse the mud off and get a drink." He suggested. She could hear the damp squeaking of his coat as he wiped his hands over it, trying to get some of the mud off of him in the thick rain. Jenny held out her hands, cupping them to collect some water. When she realized it only provided her with a small sip of water she gave up, turning her head to the sky she stuck out her tongue lapping up as much water as she could. It was delicious. Her parched mouth stung in appreciation after all of the salt water she had consumed on her swim in. She relished the pure rain water falling on her as she shivered in the dark against the chill. Soon she felt Jake's fingers tickling her arm, trying to find her in the dark.

"Alright, a bit better..." He chuckled taking her hand, "Shelter?" He asked

"Sounds good." Jenny chattered back.

In the dark she could only hope that by some small miracle they could find something sheltered from the torrent. As Jenny and Jake backed into the woods for shelter they found a small outcropping of rocks hidden under a cluster of trees that would provide them shelter from the rain and wind.

They came across it by accident when Jenny, again, stumbled on a rock, landing on the nearly dry ground underneath, "Jake." She called into the darkness.

"Here take my hand." He was instantly beside her, ready to help her to her feet.

She pulled Jake in behind her, cracking her head against the rock overhang as she tried to get into the dry space. "It's dry in here." She announced, bringing his hand with hers to the dry ground underneath them to prove it. Jake let go of her hand for a moment, feeling the dirt for himself.

"Perfect," he cheered as he pulled her in close, wary of the small amount of space their shelter provided, "this outta work."

"Plus it will keep us out of the woods... and whatever is in them." Jenny whispered darkly, still thinking of the piercing screams they had heard from within.

The area was small and Jenny tried to give Jake some space after falling asleep on him. She didn't want him to think she was, well he *was* pretty good looking, she thought. Glancing towards his shadow in the dark, she was glad he couldn't see her blushing.

He tugged her arm towards him. Sitting on the cold stone, he pulled her next to him, "We'll be warmer if we stick together." He held open his wet jacket offering her a spot next to him to stay warm, "I mean, if that's okay with you." He added when Jenny didn't answer him. After a moment she shuffled in next to him, she was trying not to read too much into his gesture, it *was* survival after all.

"Thanks." She whispered, relieved for the extra warmth in the damp chill. She still wondered though, while her mind drifted back off to sleep, what it would be like to have someone who cared for her like this in the real world. As she drifted off, Jake pulled her in closer, resting her head on his chest. He put his chin atop her head and listened to the rain pattering off of the rocks in the dark.

"Goodnight." He whispered into the night.

***

King stood at the bow of the boat, waiting as they loaded up the medical supplies and rations before departing for a third trip out to the wreckage. So far six bodies had been recovered and after thorough inspection by himself and agent Chung they had determined that their friends were still at sea.

Time was ticking and they were running low on hope as a late night storm blew in. King zipped his jacked tight, pulling on the hood for an extra measure. Behind him Chung stood still, staring listlessly into the open air, oblivious of the storm around him. The crew had wrapped themselves in plastic rain shawls to keep the water off, but within minutes the sheeting rain had them all drenched to the bone anyway.

At last the captain boarded with the last yellow watertight cooler of supplies, with a flick of a rope he was again behind the wheel and steering them back into the darkness. His radio was lively with banter from the other boats, more bags and airplane pieces were being found, no new bodies. Chung stayed silent, straining to hear the radio over the roar of the motor and the splash of the waves. To him no news was good news.

The water rocked beneath them, twisting the boat from side to side, King didn't know how the captain could steer them straight in such a storm. When they reached the site, the boats were rocking away, making it difficult to find anything in the roaring waves. Radios buzzed from other boats, talks of calling it a night until the storm passed twittered from the speakers. Chung turned with a steely eyed stare to the captain.

"We stay." He called loudly across the raging wind.

The captain watched him for a moment, his body still and impervious to the rocking of the vessel. He nodded to Chung sternly, cautious of his demeanor.

Slowly he walked to King to pull him aside, "We can stay for now, but if it gets any worse, I'm going to have to bring this boat in." He looked back to Chung with worry as water dripped down his face. Wiping it away, he turned his back to Chung, hoping he couldn't hear him, "Is he going to be okay?" He asked King sternly.

The captain was worried that Chung was about to do something rash that could put them all in danger, it was his job to keep them all safe and he didn't seem the type to take any funny business. His seriousness was conveyed to King as he looked past the captain to watch Chung himself for a moment before replying.

"I hope so." Was all he could say.

With a stern nod, the captain walked away.

CURIOUS

Grace was struggling with the fire. It seemed that as soon as it had finally started to burn nicely the rain had come down to put a damper on it, sending the small weary crowd scrambling for cover in the trees.

Grace and a small group of determined survivors were frantically trying to restart the fire. One of the others had run off to the forest to grab up as many thick leaves and fern branches as he could carry to offer them a means to protect the fire from the wind and rain. Soon they were crowded around the pile of smoldering branches, damp and shivering while holding whatever they could to stifle out the dampness from the fire as another man cautiously tried to reignite it with meticulous patience. It seemed futile, the damp had already set in and though they had tried to scavenge dry brush from the forest, it had become just as damp on the trek back to the pile.

Grace was disappointed with their progress, "Should we try to start a fire in the woods?" She asked the woman beside her, wondering if they could start something small where it was dry, "We could move it out here once it gets started?" She added, the woman looked to her in the darkness, frowning as she contemplated Grace's idea. She passed her leaves to Grace with a smile.

"That's a great idea honey, I'll tell Jacob." She knelt next to the man with the lighter, whispering to him in the darkness. Soon he was standing and walking into the woods, the woman turned to address the leaf holders, "We are going to try to start the fire in the woods where it's dry, try to cover the wood from the rain so we can move it out here after." She was firm in her words, taking her leaves back from Grace she began to place them like shingles on the small stack of wood. Within minutes the others had joined, soon their pile was protected.

Night had fallen and grown deeper in the hours it had taken to start the smoldering pile of coals. Grace watched the shore with tired eyes, through the darkness and sheets of rain, for a light in the distance. Their rescue had been put on hold, she was sure of it. The weather would affect their search efforts, hindering their ability to pinpoint the survivors. By the time they found the wreckage it would have washed away from the island. Without their signal fire they were lost.

Grace struggled to find dry timber to start a smaller fire under the cover of the trees. There was no sense in letting the flames die out and no sense in being cold for the night. She paced into the dark woods, keeping the dim embers of the bonfire in sight to guide her back to the others. If she wandered too far she might not be able to find a way back. So she stuck close, weaving sightlessly through the trees and brambles with a grace that only a true survivor could possess. It reminded her of her run through the woods back when her father had been chasing her.

Her father. She hadn't thought of him since the message he had left on her phone. Life had been too busy to care when she discovered he had been murdered in prison. She stopped for a moment to dwell on the loss.

She wasn't sure what emotions were proper for her to feel about him. She tried to sort through what she really felt and what she thought her therapist would want her to feel. In reality she was disappointed that he hadn't been able to tell her the vital clues he had held. She was jealous that she didn't know all of his little secrets, but she was not sad. She knew if she hadn't been on her way to a safe house she would have been expected to attend a service for him. Not that she cared, but because there was no one else in the whole world that would want to mourn him.

Suddenly she felt pity for him, alone in his final moments, with not a single person who truly cared. His life had been worse than hers after all.

She looked up, smiling at the place in the stars, thought she could not see them, that her father had once called home. That was when she saw it; in the tree above her there was a blink of red. She froze believing it to be the glare off the eye of an animal. She feared there was a predator in the area and her body tensed.

She listened, no sound came from the red blinking glow. It looked like a light in the otherwise untamed forest. *Strange*, she thought. She took a tentative step closer, ready to jump back if it moved. Water dripped from her hair into her eyes. Slowly she brushed the droplets away, wary of the light and what the source might be. It remained stationary, just above her head. It was within her reach so she held her hand up tentatively, afraid it might jump at her. Moving her hand forward slowly she brushed her fingers against the red light as it lit up again.

She felt metal, cool and damp against her hand, the round smooth glass of the lens.

A camera in the woods.

Grace was curious, sure this was probably a private island with a hidden cottage for some rich stock market guru, but why would there be cameras in the woods? How many trespassers had come before them that it was necessary? She picked up the small pile of branches that she had gathered and walked towards the embers to talk to Jerry about it. She hunched over the wood to keep it from the rain. Hastily, she traced her steps back to the others, protecting the wood from the dampness as best as she could.

Something about the island seemed suspicious to Grace and as she raced across the beach she knew that Jerry would be willing to talk about it in private without worrying the others. It seemed odd that a small island like this would need security cameras. If there were functional cameras, they might be able to use them to call for help if it didn't arrive soon. The thought left her torn between curiosity and elation. If someone on the island had the know how to use the camera parts to get them help it would be wonderful, but why were there cameras?

The woods were dark and even with the glowing embers marking her destination, it didn't help her through the woods safely, tree roots and low brush clung at her clothing and the wood in her hand. She stumbled, toppling the pile onto the ground before her. Blindly she reached out, dropping to her knees to feel at the muddy earth for the twigs she had so desperately piled. Her knee was stinging from something she had tangled with in the woods. She felt her pants with her fingers.

A large rip in the fabric told her she had nicked herself good. She gathered the rest of the wood quietly, watching the embers ahead, she wasn't far off. From the ground level she could see the shadows of more obstacles in her way, overhead a beeping sounded. She looked up startled. Quickly standing with her handful of wood, she made her way as hastily and cautiously as possible out of the dangerous woods. Something was really off. She felt a shiver roll up her spine, like someone was watching her. Moving faster, she bit her tongue as she walked into another log. She needed to get out of the watching woods and back to the safety of the crowd.

Grace was quick to dump her armful of twigs as she reached the waiting crowd. Already someone had gathered some embers from the outer fire to start their small warming pile inside the dry woods. They were grateful for the addition to the pile as it slowly smoked, amassing a small fire that glowed. It lit the chattering crown and provided a small amount of warmth. Grace stepped back from the fire as her damp wood began to cause a smoke screen, scanning the crowd quickly for a sign of Jerry before the smoke overtook the small clearing impeding her vision. She hadn't seen him among the others. Slowly she retreated to the beach in search.

She found Jerry on the beach sitting in the rain on the other side of the dying fire. He was staring at the coast and the debris that were still washing ashore. She tapped him gently, frowning at him for wandering into the rain alone. He would surely catch a cold from this, but she was glad to catch him alone. His clothing clung to him as the sheets of rain fell from the sky. She watched him chattering, worried that it was already too late to warm him back up.

Her hair fell in her face again, dripping wet from the storm, she wished she had worn it up. She tapped Jerry on the shoulder again, drawing his attention from the dark waves. She couldn't see what he was watching, but the wet slapping told her something was washing ashore ahead of them.

"Jerry, could you come with me? I found something in the woods, I wanted to show you. It's very curious." She added, knowing it would entice him to come if he thought it would be a mystery for him to solve. He would only leave the beach if he was needed to help. Grace knew he would help her find the source of the cameras, or give her an idea of how to use them to their advantage. She listened to the waves while she waited, hoping to hear a motor over the pattering rain and slapping waves, nothing caught her ear. She frowned at the thought of Jerry staying overnight on this island, she knew he was on medications, he had packed nearly a whole bag of the stuff. She didn't know if he could go a full day without taking it, she was worried.

"Oh, I didn't see you there." Jerry turned slowly in the sand to look up at Grace, as he stood she watched him shaking. She held out her hand to steady him against the raging storm. He was in really bad shape.

"Here." Grace put an arm around Jerry's shaking frame, hoping to warm him in the chilly damp.

"What was it you wanted to show me?" He asked slowly as though he were having trouble placing his thoughts.

"I saw something in the woods, a blinking light." She turned to the woods again, trying to remember where she had seen the light. It was hard to pinpoint in the dark. She guessed the direction and started walking.

"Blinking lights? How curious..." Jerry was slow on his feet, stumbling through the dark lumpy terrain of the beach. Grace held him firmly as she walked forward.

Jerry followed Grace into the woods. Damp and dripping they walked to the spot where she had seen the flashing red light. When Grace looked up to pinpoint it, she realized there were more, spreading throughout the forest, visible only in the black dark of the night upon them. There were flashing red lights throughout the trees and beyond.

This was more than a security system.

Above them the closest camera flashed red sporadically, making a beeping sound above their heads. Grace watched with concern. Were they being watched?

RECOGNITION

Ethan stood transfixed while Bruce paced in the dark, "Who would do that? How did it happen?" He turned to Ethan, his mouth was opening and closing as he tried to find the words. Finally it slowed as he began to think logically, "Did you hear anything?" He was close enough to see the shadow of Ethan's face. Ethan nodded, not sure if Bruce could see him, he spoke.

"Yes, I heard footsteps in the woods. They came in slowly, but after the fire started they ran, back behind me." He pointed, letting his hand drop when he realized they couldn't see him. The other man stood with effort. Ethan didn't remember his name, it might have been Jim, or Dan. One of them was lying on the forest floor. He felt a little guilty for not knowing which was which.

The smoldering woods smelled like wet burnt flesh and leaves, an unfavorable combination that caused his stomach to churn as his mind thought about what had happened. Ethan held a hand to his mouth as the taste of bile overwhelmed his senses. Finally he couldn't hold it in any longer, turning to the tree behind him he wretched up what was left in his empty stomach.

"Are you okay?" Bruce asked from behind him, placing a hand on his back.

Ethan took a deep breath, holding himself still while the sick sensation washed over him. "Yeah." He replied thickly.

"Do you think it was one of the others? From the beach?" Bruce was talking to the others now, giving Ethan a moment to settle his stomach.

"Who would do something like that?" Asked one of them shakily.

"Why would they run off?" Asked another.

Ethan stood slowly as his stomach returned to normal. He turned to the clearing where the others sat, cowering at the base of a tree as far from the smoldering body as they could muster. He breathed deeply through his mouth, avoiding the stench of the body, almost tasting it in his haste for fresh air. It was a gruesome way to go and he couldn't fathom who would do such an atrocious thing to another human.

He stared at the small glowing red embers where the word had formed. He hoped he was wrong, but it certainly was curious. Was this another set up?

How could it be, they were on their way to a safe house. No one should have been able to intercept them on their way. The plane crash seemed a fluke accident, but now he wondered; the whole thing reeked of Colt. He began to panic in his head, wondering if he should go back to Grace and let her know, or if she was even safe while he was wandering in the woods, separated from her. She could have faced some other form of evil and what of Jenny, was she a lost cause? His brain flashed the worst case scenarios before him as he stood transfixed, paralyzed when he thought each one through.

"What is that?" Jim or Dan asked, obviously pointing at something. It broke Ethan's thought, he snapped his head up to look.

"Where, I can't see what you are pointing at?" Ethan reminded him of the darkness, scanning the forest for whatever he might be looking at.

"Up in the tree, I thought I saw a flash of red, like a light." A crunching sounded, approaching Ethan. He held out his hands before he was trampled on, "Oh sorry." Jim or Dan apologized as he stepped onto Ethan's foot. Ethan winced.

"It's okay, which way was the light?" He asked, now that Jim or Dan was close enough to show him. He reached for Ethan's hand, holding it upwards with his own, he aimed their hands together towards a tree above them.

"There," he said positively, "it's flashing."

Ethan turned his head to follow his hand, letting his arm drop back to his side when he saw it.

It was unmistakable in the forest, unnatural looking against the trees. He wondered how he hadn't noticed it before. A small red flashing light, much like the ones in the security cameras he used at his home, he frowned. Suddenly his mind was on fire with possibilities, reasons to explain why there would be a security camera hidden in the dense woods.

"We should see what it is." He walked forward to where he might assume the trunk of the tree was, not quite convinced that it was in fact a camera. He was off by a few inches and walked into a bush, his hands didn't break his stumble. When he finally found the trunk of the tree, he followed the branch upwards, feeling slowly towards the light flashing above him.

He could see shadows now, the storm must have blown over. The rain had died down and it was getting a little easier to see, dawn was approaching.

Using his hands outstretched above his head, he traced the damp bark towards the light. When he reached the object with the light he brushed it over with his hand cautiously. It was metallic and cool to his touch. Damp even, from the earlier storm. Grasping it tightly he gave it a tug, it was stuck tight. He reached up to use two hands, pulling with strain. It was a small camera, fitting easily into the palm of one hand and it wasn't budging. His hands slipped on the slick metal and he stumbled back into a bush.

"It's a camera." He announced to the others, who hadn't been able to see his struggle with the branches. He stood up, brushing himself off as quietly as possible to cover his embarrassing blunder.

Bruce sounded pissed, growling into the dark, "Why on earth would there be cameras on this island? Are we on some reality show or something? We'd better not be on some reality show. They just burned Jim alive. That's messed up." Ethan could see his outline, pacing in the woods. The one who must be Dan walked towards him, unnerved at the thought that they were being watched.

"That's pretty messed up, we'd better get to the others quick and then head back to the beach. I don't want to spend too much time in these woods, especially if they're bugged." He started looking for the landmark they had erected when nightfall had stopped their excursion short. When he found it he started walking, "This way." He called over his shoulder as he led the way out of their small clearing and away from the smoldering prone form of his companion. After a few steps he turned back, sorrow washing over his unseen face.

"Should we take him with us?" He asked slowly as the others crossed the clearing to follow him into dawn.

"I don't know if we can carry him." Bruce was remorseful. Leaving the burnt man alone in the woods seemed cruel, crueler than his demise even. It would be near impossible to find him again if they did leave him, if scavengers hadn't found him by then, there was also the fact that they had not followed a traceable path to get to the clearing. If they left his body alone in the woods, there was no way to retrieve it later. Ethan thought the predicament over for a moment, standing still and silent in the woods with the others as they contemplated the possibilities. No one would want to carry the smoldering body on their shoulders, the heat and the stench alone; not to mention it would slow them down considerably.

Slowly Ethan stepped to the marker they had placed in the ground to mark their path. With a gentle tug he pulled it from the ground, scanning the area in the dim light for other loose sticks that were sizable enough to create a makeshift stretcher. By the time he had amassed a couple more pieces, Bruce was at his side watching intently.

"Stretcher?" He asked, reaching for another stick off of the forest floor. Ethan nodded.

"I think it'll be the easiest way." He set his pile of materials on the ground as Dan walked back into the clearing to help.

Soon they had created a stretcher for Jim's body, using sticks and vines with the addition of articles of clothing that they were able to sacrifice to give it some stability; a sock here, a shoelace there. Once Jim's body had been properly secured, Ethan reached for the front handles and Dan turned to lead the way out of the woods.

Ethan followed the sound of his footfalls, with his hands tied behind him holding the stretcher steady, hoping to avoid crashing into anything. Dan and Bruce took off ahead. They seemed determined to put as much space between them and the smell of rotting flesh as quickly as possible.

The dim light of morning provided a small amount of relief to Ethan racing after Bruce and Dan in the dense woods. He struggled to weave his way through the brambles and branches with the same finesse as the two in the lead while carrying the stretcher behind him. He caught himself more than once on something sharp, his shirt was ripped in several place. Soon the brambles were starting to snag on his skin, tearing open several sizable gashes on his abdomen as he fought to keep pace. He wasn't about to get left behind out in the watchful woods.

As he raced after Bruce, his mind wandered to the others, to Colt, to King and Chung, swirling up scenarios in his head where everything went wrong and scenarios where he fought back. He dare not let the others know what he thought was going on, the fear he felt was enough to keep him going, he couldn't let them know what they might be up against.

Soon Ethan's struggle with the stretcher became too much, he and the others had fallen behind. Looping back, Dan grasped the stretcher out of his tired arms and again sped off through the woods as though he were running on adrenalin, nothing was slowing him down.

Ethan struggled to keep up. Even with the dead weight Dan was hauling, he was quick to pass through the thick woods. In his tired and bloody state, Ethan easily lost sight of him again and again as he struggled against his chronic asthma and stiff joints.

Two of the others trailed behind Ethan, gasping as they tried to keep up to him and ahead he was losing sight of Dan again as he led the way to freedom. It was getting lighter with the dawn, but still not light enough to see very well. Adrenalin coursed through his veins, fighting off the hunger and thirst that would normally have prevented him from continuing on. This was a matter of survival.

***

He watched them with fascination, unable to see much through the black screens. He should have put up some night time feeds, but the banter through the microphones was enough to tell him they were catching on. Slowly, but they were catching on. It had taken them a bit longer this time. They had wasted more time than he had anticipated, waiting for a rescue to happen. By dawn they would be gone and he would be safe on his boat on route to the safe house he had arranged to wait out the backlash. No one would ever have to know otherwise, no one would ever know he was here. He sat back, watching their progress through the woods.

His phone beeped in his pocket, he pulled it out swiping the touch screen to answer.

"Hello." He said with pride.

"Is it done?" Asked the raspy voice on the other end.

"It will be by tomorrow." He was getting excited now.

"Don't toy with them Colt, just get it done."

Colt frowned, "It will be done." He clicked the line. What good was it if he didn't have a chance to toy with them? He had been looking forward to this moment for years. He was going to enjoy it.

He set the phone on his desk, reaching underneath for the small duffel bag he had stashed during his prep work. Dry clothes greeted him as he pulled the zipper across.

"Perfect." He whispered to himself as he changed.

With the three of them separated, he was in good fortune. He couldn't have wished for the crash to go any better than it had. Asides from a stiff ankle, he himself had fared well. Luckily he had escaped before the actual crash, but they needn't know that when they came to the rescue.

He imagined the agents had been informed already. They had probably already selected out their new cavalry. But they wouldn't make it in time and if they did he would be waiting with open arms; fire arms that is. He chuckled at the thought of them racing in to find his mess.

He sat back in his chair, watching the dark monitors with anticipation.

It was going to be spectacular.

ACCEPTANCE

Grace stood still in the forest staring up at the flashing red light. It cast a
dim glow into the night. Not enough to see much, but enough to give her a
small silhouette of the item it was attached to if she stared at it long enough.
A small shape nestled into the tree, it blinked off and on for a moment,
then it held its light, dim red, she turned away. Was someone watching her?

When she had shown it to Jerry and he had gone silent she had
started to worry. She waited with bated breath, listening to the sound of his
labored breathing, fearful that he had taken a stroke or something worse.
She watched his silhouette carefully for signs of distress wondering why he
wasn't speaking. He stared up at the tree as though frozen on the spot. She
wondered what he was thinking, turning to the light herself to imagine what
he would think of a camera in the woods.

Was he trying to figure out how to rewire it to call for help? Was he
imagining tracing it to the source? She stared back towards him waiting for
an answer.

She was still standing silently when the first dim sign of dawn
began to appear on the horizon. Reaching out, she grasped Jerry's hand,
squeezing it tightly.

"Jer. Are you okay?"

Jerry stared at the light in shock. No one would waste money equipping a private island with cameras, especially not out in the dense woods. What could it be watching for? He stared beyond the light to the others, blinking in the distance. No one would waste their time with this many cameras on a deserted island and by all accounts this was a remote island, uninhabited, or they would have found help by now. He kept his composure as his mind spun with the possibility that they were in fact in great danger having survived the crash.

"Just thinking, Grace....just thinking for a moment..." He replied, slowly trailing off as he continued to stare into the woods at the other lights and then back up to the one in the tree above them.

Jerry was panicked, Ethan had wandered off into the woods with a rag-tag crew of strangers. One of them could very well be Colt. He assumed that was the purpose of the cameras. Much like the amusement park, they were being watched and led through his obstacles. He didn't know what to say, he didn't know what to think. He could feel his heart racing in his chest, hear it pounding in his ears, his breath caught in his throat.

Jerry had a feeling Colt was not going to let them out unscathed this time. Somehow he had managed to get them alone and without the help of the outside world. Jerry didn't know if they could manage now that they had been separated. If he and Grace had been with Ethan and Jenny, they would have stood a chance, as a whole they were strong.

He let his mind wander for a moment longer. He watched the flashing of the red light silently, wondering if there were microphones in the trees as well. It didn't make much sense for a normal person to cover their island in cameras, so it seemed reasonable and rational for his mind to immediately wander to Colt. He was who they were on their way into hiding from after all. What if he had gotten to them before King could get them to safety? The man had an underlying intelligence and he seemed to know the system. He had been trained by Hart and from what he knew of Hart they were in for trouble.

Jerry looked at Grace, seeing only her outline. She looked so much like her mother now that she had grown up. He bit his lip to keep his thoughts in. How could he tell her that Ethan was in danger without putting her in danger? She was such a strong headed woman she would surely chase after him, or would she stay with him to watch over her senile friend?

He stared at the flashing lights for a moment longer, the woods were beginning to brighten before he spoke. He chose his words gently "Grace, this isn't normal." He pointed up to the camera, "No one puts up this many cameras unless they have something to hide from....or they are watching for something....I think it might be Colt..." He looked to her confused face, she was wide eyed in the mornings dim light. Her eyes reflected the red flashes as she gaped, her mouth wide.

"How is that possible? We were going to a safe house. No one should have known where we were, besides, how could he have all this set up if we didn't even know where we were going?" She shrugged her shoulders, believing she had just debunked his conspiracy theory, quickly growing quiet as she thought about the circumstances. She pulled her arms in, wrapping them around her chest for comfort as she began to shake.

He turned to her with a serious face that she recognized as his *I have bad news* face, she paused. Rethinking what she had just said, she repeated it slower, "How could he have all this set up if we didn't even know where we were going?" Her face went white.

"Grace." He walked closer and lowered his voice, covering his mouth to muffle his speech as Ethan had told him he had done at the amusement park, "What if that wasn't the safe house King had in mind.

Would they really have the paperwork sorted through that fast? They would have barely had time to get back before that package arrived..." He lowered his hand, watching as her eyes grew ever wider.

Hearing the words spoken out loud made it more believable to him. He had been teetering on disbelief himself, but the more he thought it through the more he believed it to be Colt. King and Chung would have insisted that they go into hiding closer to them, Florida was very out of the way.

"This is a trap?" She whispered quizzically into the silent forest. That was when she realized the truth. If this was a setup then they were in for a lot more trouble. She was surprised that more hadn't happened if Colt was watching them.

"Ethan," she whispered, staring up at Jerry's face as white as a ghost, "and Jenny." Her lip quivered at the thought of them, alone on the island.

If he had them trapped on an island, it seemed suspicious that it hadn't been more eventful. Then again, Ethan and Jenny were out there all alone, separated from her and Jerry. They could be in danger at that very moment and Grace was unable to help. Could she really trust the people Ethan had left the beach with? Was he safe? And where was Jenny in all of this?

"I shouldn't have let Ethan go alone, we should have gone together to get Jenny." She said quietly while she sat on the damp ground. She moved slowly as her head spun at the thought that they were trapped.

Maybe help wasn't coming.

"Ethan will find Jenny, if she is out there..." Jerry sounded as though he were trying to convince himself.

"What about the people with him?" Grace whispered the thought quietly, wondering if Ethan would be able to defend himself if one of the others were working with Colt, or perhaps *was* Colt.

Overhead the beeping became more frequent, "I think he's watching." Jerry whispered, crouching next to her. They both knew that it was a sign that the games had begun. As psychotic as Colt was, he wouldn't kill them unless they knew it was him. Their conversation would have to wait.

Now they were in danger.

Grace looked to Jerry with pleading, tired, eyes, "Then let the games begin..." She whispered.

Standing slowly, she took Jerry's hand and led him out of the watching woods.

DANGER

Dan led them through the wilderness at a tiring pace. They raced after him as he jumped through bushes and over fallen logs, panting as they struggled. He was in a hurry to find the tail end of the plane and whatever survivors it may have held.

The trees were more than just obstacles as they blocked Ethan's sight of their assumed leader several times, sending him racing after to catch up. Behind him the others were falling even farther behind

"Wait up." They called and Ethan slowed his pace, trying to keep Bruce in his sight, while Dan and the stretcher took off unseen. Ethan stared ahead at Bruce, he wasn't about to let the forest consume him as well.

"Bruce." He called forward into the trees. He watched as Bruce hesitated for a moment, turning back to search for the person calling for him. With a jolt he was gone as Dan tugged at the stretcher, sending them through another tangle of bushes.

Ethan raced forward, trying to keep them in sight as he struggled to breath in the damp morning air. He tackled his way through the underbrush listening to the crunching and dragging of Dan and Bruce ahead of him, trying to determine which direction they had gone.

Behind him the others had grown silent, no pleading for Ethan to slow down, or sounds of the brush snapping as they struggled to keep up. They must have fallen farther behind, Ethan reasoned as he pushed forward with the last of his energy.

Within a minute he was fatigued, queasy and short of breath. He slowed to a walk to recover as his concern for the travelers behind him grew. Had they taken a wrong turn? Was one of them injured? How were Dan and Bruce keeping up at such a fast pace? Would they slow down when they realized they had lost the others?

Heavy breathing sounded behind him. He froze, standing as still as he could muster with his aching muscles. He breathed out slowly, listening to the forest around him, wondering if it was the others catching up that had startled him.

"Hello?" He whispered, hopeful for a reply. He turned slowly as the breathing came again, hoarse and ragged like a panting dog that had been in the heat for too long. "Is someone there?" He whispered even quieter, suddenly aware that his heart was beating faster.

A growl came from the bush at his heels. The hair on the back of his neck raised as a chill rolled down his spine. Without a backwards glance, he charged forward through the forest away from the sound. Ethan raced through the forest faster, fearful of what may be behind him in the brush.

Finally he could see Bruce not far ahead of him. With a ragged breath, he heaved himself through the brush towards the moving figure ahead.

There was screaming and a loud resonating bang, muffled cries erupted from within the trees. Ethan ducked as he turned his head towards the sound, racing forward, wondering if he should go back to investigate. More screaming sounded behind him, pained and wailing. He quickened his pace as Bruce looked back.

"Something is following us." Ethan gasped over heaving breaths of air as he closed in on Bruce. The two were tiring quickly, but now they couldn't slow down. Something was catching up and they needed to put as much space between them and the heavy breathing beast as possible.

"Go faster." Bruce yelled ahead to Dan in a panic.

Dan took off like a rocket with the stretcher in his hands, dragging Bruce along with him through the woods. Ethan struggled to keep close behind.

It was close on their heels, a crackling of branches and a panting breath that came at their heels. Ethan pressed forward, keeping pace with Bruce at the rear of the stretcher as Dan plowed through the trees ahead leading the way.

Fear coursed through his body as he crashed through the brush, the sound was finally growing distant. A howl sounded behind them in the distance. Still, they pressed forward, resolved to put as much forest between them and the animal as they could possibly muster.

"Where are the others?" Bruce panted to Ethan as he continued after Dan, still clutching the stretcher that pulled him forward.

Ethan didn't have time to answer.

There was a rumbling and Ethan was tossed back, slamming into the damp bark of a tree. He slid down, collapsing against the forest floor. Pieces of debris sprinkled his face as he shook the ringing from his ears. He struggled to his feet, aching from head to toe and wondering what had happened.

He stumbled over to Bruce who was beside him in a heap. Bruce rolled over looking horrified. His hand pointed to where Dan had been only a moment before, a crater in the ground had replaced their companion. Ethan didn't see him, he brushed the dirt from his face, it felt damp. He looked at his hand, it was covered in blood. He searched for Dan across the now clear area. There was a dark crater and a splattering of debris covering the forest, but no Dan, no stretcher, no one. Finally Ethan looked upwards, wondering how far the sudden blast had radiated. In the tree above the crater there was a tattered bloody shoe.

Ethan froze, "What happened?" He yelled over the ringing in his ears. He didn't really care who heard him, somehow Dan had been thrashed into a million pieces before him. He was afraid to move. He sat slowly at the base of the tree mesmerized by the sight before him. The forest had been painted red, it dripped from trees and bushes as though it were Halloween decor gone awry.

Bruce stood carefully, looking around cautiously as he placed his feet back onto the damp earth, "I think it was a land mine or something..." His eyes were wide, looking for some other reasonable answer, land mines in their path was obviously a worst case scenario. He looked wildly around before repeating his previous thought, "I think it was a land mine." With more belief.

Bruce reached up to touch his face, splinters of wood clung to his features, an indication of what had become of the stretcher. He winced as he pulled out a small fragment, carefully patting down the rest of his body. Finally he sighed with relief, thankful for only a few small scrapes and cuts given the tattered state of Dan.

"What is going on here?" He turned to Ethan now, confusion on his furrowed brow, "It's like we're trapped in a horror movie..." He trailed off scanning the scene before turning to stare at Ethan with wide eyes.

Ethan stared back at him, his mind wandering as he watched Bruce, his only companion in a forest of horrors. He had said it well, it was like they had been thrust into a horror movie, cameras and all.

"Ethan?" Bruce was watching him carefully now. Ethan realized he was staring back, blank faced. The ringing in his ears had yet to subside, Bruce sounded like he was far away and underwater.

"Yeah." Ethan finally answered, calling across the dripping clearing to the tree Bruce had wandered towards. They both looked at the scene one more time, contemplating the dangers before them

"How do we get through? What if there's more than one?" Ethan asked, knowing that Bruce was thinking the same thing.

"This is crazy." Bruce spoke slowly, wiping more of the debris and blood from his face as he looked around, standing as close to the base of the trees as he could manage without knocking himself over.

"There has to be a way though." Ethan commented, searching for an alternate route. He was unsure if there were more land mines or if their path was now clear, he wasn't sure he was willing to risk his life to find out either. He looked up for an answer, staring through the crimson trees to the little bit of morning light that was filtering through.

Bruce followed his gaze, "Looks like we're playing monkeys." He decided as he pointed upwards to the red trees. He turned back to regard Ethan, bloodied and shaken.

"Monkeys?" Ethan looked down, confused.

"Swinging from tree to tree, it'll keep us off the ground," Bruce pointed upwards at the thick sturdy branches overhead, "I don't think I want to find out if there are any more mines..." He trailed off dropping his hand to his side as he felt for the first aid kit in his pocket, somehow it comforted him to know it was still there.

"I guess that could work." Ethan was smirking now, he would never have thought of a crazy plan like that. He was about to suggest hopping from tree root to tree root, maybe finding some rocks to toss ahead of them to set off any mines that might be in the vicinity. Bruce was a genius.

"Where are the others?" Bruce asked with confusion, scanning the area for more fallen comrades, believing they may have taken cover from the blast. Ethan looked behind him, into the undamaged forest, trying to hear the crackle of footsteps over the deafening ring in his ears.

"I don't know, they fell behind a while ago..." Ethan glanced at Bruce watching him staring into the woods, wondering if he was having any more luck locating them in the thick trees.

"I told Dan to slow down..." Bruce was quiet now, Ethan could barely hear his comment. Bruce looked back up at the dangling shoe. "They're probably lost by now."

"There was something behind me when we were running, heavy breathing. I ran faster... there was screaming, I ran..." Ethan admitted sheepishly.

"Screaming?" Bruce asked.

"Screaming in the woods behind me, before the...thing....came chasing after us."

"Do you think they're hurt?" Bruce asked slowly, "Do you think it got them?"

"I don't even know what *it* was..." Ethan shook his head apologetically, "I never actually saw anything..."

"I thought I heard something crashing behind us after you caught up," Bruce shook his head, "I just thought it was the others. If it wasn't them, then that thing was right behind us..."

"It could still be there." Ethan agreed.

"Do you think the others will catch up?"

"Should we wait for them?" Ethan asked, hopeful that Bruce wouldn't be stupid enough to turn around in this forest after discovering the land mine. There was a good chance there were more of them out there waiting to be triggered.

"Uh, I don't know," he called loudly through the ear ringing as he wiped blood from his face, "I would feel bad leaving them, but what if there are more explosives?" It appeared he had thought the same as Ethan.

"How about we just wait a few minutes instead, wipe some of this blood off, scan the trees for good branches, maybe they'll catch up?" Ethan suggested finally. He stayed at the base of the tree he had been thrown against, knowing it would be nearly impossible to dig a land mine into the trees roots.

Bruce nodded, reaching up slowly he grabbed hold of a branch overhead, pulling himself up with effort. Once his feet were off the ground he swung around trying to keep them off the forest floor while he struggled to right himself on the branch. Ethan watched him, scanning the tree at his back for a similar escape route from the ground. Bruce was clever to wait up where the ground couldn't explode on him and the beast couldn't reach him. Finally Bruce settled and Ethan began his climb up into the adjacent tree.

Together they sat silently for what felt like an eternity, scanning the forest which was now obstructing them from a brilliant view with bushes and trees covered in gore. They couldn't see very far into the wood at all. Ethan strained to hear through the trees when the ringing in his ears finally subsided. He listened for rustling or voices, anything that would let him know if the others were coming. He also searched through the brush for movement, wary of the growling thing that had spurred them on earlier, leaving them moments before the explosion. Had the animal sensed something in the woods that they had not, was there an animal at all?

"See anything yet?" He called to Bruce.

"Nothing yet. Just a few more minutes?" Bruce asked, still picking splinters from his arms and neck.

"Sure thing." Ethan turned to watch the forest ahead of them for a moment, looking for a viable way through the trees and perhaps hoping secretly to catch a glimpse of a camera. He couldn't shake the feeling that they were still being watched. The fiery word that had trailed across the forest floor clung to his mind as he searched for blinking red lights. With the morning light breaking through the branches overhead he finally gave up, the lights had been quite visible in the night, he probably couldn't find any now.

He tensed on the branch as his muscles seized, he was afraid of falling. Though the ground was only a few feet away from him, he didn't trust that it was safe. *Only a few more minutes*, he told himself as he sat stiffly in the tree, *then we can get going*.

He would feel bad leaving the others behind, but he wasn't about to leave Jenny out alone on an island that appeared to be run by a savage. If she was on the island then she was surely facing similar danger and he cared more about her than two strangers that he had survived a plane crash with any day.

Ethan was about to give up, exchanging looks of *let's get going* silently with Bruce across the bloody clearing when he heard a crackling somewhere behind Bruce. They both turned to listen as it slowly grew closer, a scraping of leaves and the muffled whimpers of someone crying.

There was a dragging and a whimpering as the bushes began to rattle in the distance.

"That's them." Bruce called across to Ethan.

"Are you sure?"

"I'm sure...Just wait." Bruce perked up in his tree, watching intently while the shuffling grew closer, the whimpering more defined. It was human, the distant whisper of chatter carried towards them, still too far away for them to define the words that were being spoken.

Ethan leaned forward wondering what was keeping them, they

were moving at a snail's pace through the underbrush. Every now and then he could catch a glimpse of the top of a head, or a hand, but they were still too far away. He was growing anxious, knowing that every moment he wasted waiting on them he was leaving Jenny alone; and Grace and Jerry. He needed to speed this up.

Finally the rustling grew close enough that they could hear the whisper of voices clearly.

"Just keep going." Sobbed one.

"I am, it's my ankle." Said another.

Bruce looked back to Ethan with wide eyes quickly before he turned to call out.

"Hey, who's there?" He hollered through the empty forest. Ethan froze atop his branch, wondering if the growling thing that had been behind him earlier was in the vicinity. He tightened his grip on the branches beneath him as he listened, hopeful that it would not return.

"Bruce, be careful, what if that animal is still out there." He called as quietly as he could across the tree.

The scraping grew closer, Bruce turned towards Ethan with wide eyes again. They could see the others heads bobbing through the trees, they were close together. Ethan searched the other bushes for rustling, fearful that the animal was still out there.

Bruce had other concerns, glancing back at the catastrophe behind him, his eyes grew wide with fear. Twisting his head slowly towards the noise in the bushes he called out, "Get off the ground!" As loud as he could muster, his voice crackled. "Shit." He whispered to Ethan as the shuffling sound grew closer.

"Guys?" A small far away voice called back,

"Is that you?" Called another.

It was the stragglers in the woods, finding their way slowly back into the pack. But what was the dragging sound? Ethan craned his neck to see over the branches. He could finally see them coming into view, one small hunched shape dragging another.

"Get off the ground!" Ethan called out to them urgently.

"Get in the trees!" Bruce pleaded as they pulled themselves closer. It looked like one was dragging a body, limp and trailing blood. Something had gone awry in the woods and they were stupid enough to be putting everyone in danger by staying on the forest floor.

"We can't," shouted the small voice again, "Devon is hurt!" It called to them, dragging the body closer, "Someone shot at us." He yelled again, coming closer still.

"Get off the ground!" Bruce howled as they came closer to the bloodied forest surrounding them. "There are land mines!" He shouted louder, they continued to close in on the clearing.

Ethan clung to the branch tightly closing his eyes, ready for a blast as the dragging came closer and closer. They would have to leave the injured Devon if they hoped to survive. The only safe way was through the trees and his limp body would slow them down.

Bruce was still screaming at them when it happened. This time Ethan had been prepared. The forest shook beneath him, debris pelted at his back and side. He clung on, eyes closed. This time he was far enough away.

As the blast subsided Ethan opened his eyes, hopeful that Bruce would still be with him, afraid for a moment of being in the woods alone. Ethan scanned the tree where Bruce had been, empty branches shook in the aftermath of the blow. For a moment Ethan could feel the panic creeping through him, until a gruff cough below led him to Bruce, crumpled against the roots of a tree, otherwise he seemed alright.

"Well that sucked." He coughed, looking up for a branch to pull himself back onto. Bruce reached again for a low hanging branch without moving his feet on the ground. Bruce struggled, lifting one foot at a time as he pulled with tired arms, trying to right himself on the small branch. Ethan watched with anxiety as Bruce teetered between success and failure, more than once losing his grip and nearly catapulting back to the ground. Finally he had righted himself on a stronger branch.

"They're gone." Ethan whispered across the clearing, searching for a sign of life among the falling leaves and debris in the forest where they had been.

"I tried to warn them..." Bruce was pale. He sat stiffly on his branch, shaking in the light morning breeze.

They couldn't stay on the forest floor if it was set to kill them, but they still needed to get out. Knowing that they had nothing left to lose, the two silently agreed to continue. It was a shame that they had lost the others in the woods, but as Ethan had thought bitterly before, he cared more about Jenny and Grace and Jerry than he did the strangers from the plane. He had to make it back alive, or die trying.

Slowly the two began to climb from one tree to the next, careful not to touch the forest floor, it was tedious work. They swung from one branch to another while keeping their feet clear of the forest floor as they tried to remember which way they were heading. Often they found themselves having to go around in a loop before finding a tree that could support them in the direction they wanted to go.

Ethan listened over the crackling and rustling of the branches for signs of human life ahead, or signs of impending doom. He assumed most of the island was now as deadly as the amusement park had been and beyond his own labored breathing it was hard to hear much of anything in the forest around him. His arms burned as he climbed on ahead following Bruce in their twisted path forwards, at least he thought it was forwards.

RELIEF

Jenny awoke, warm and shivering all at the same time. Jake was still sleeping, wrapped around her for warmth. She shifted his weight back towards the rocks, knowing that she should excuse herself to find an area to use for her natural functions, suddenly feeling quite awkward.

When she stood from under the rock's overhang the dim light of morning washed over her. Instantly she was warm again, the bright sun filtered through the leaves and she could finally see where she was. She stood at the edge of an expanse of forest that she could see no end to. Somewhere close by was the cliff face, but the brush was so thick she couldn't see it, just the vastness of sky beyond the edge of the forest, painted orange as the waiting sun rose from below.

The view was spectacular. She thought of all the cheesy post cards her brother would send her from curious places with imagery of sunsets and reflective lakes surrounded by pines. She wished she could capture the scene before her to show him one day, one day when she was back home and safe.

She heard a rustling in the forest, not that far off. She started towards it wondering if the others had made it onto the island. Then she paused, it could be an animal.

She had walked away from the noise to relieve herself when the eruption happened. She whipped her head to look at the trees, the deafening blast shook the ground and she could see in the treetops that the epicenter was not far off.

It sounded like something in the forest had exploded. She pulled herself up awkwardly and raced back to Jake to alert him. They might be in danger. Or perhaps, she thought afterward, a rescue party was out there looking for them and it was just a flare backfiring in the forest while they searched. She slowed her pace when she reached the area where they had sheltered themselves from the storm, searching through the undergrowth for the fluke hiding spot her shins had found in the dead of night. It was harder to find than she had thought, rummaging about the bushes, she searched for Jake.

"Jake?" She whispered, starting to worry that she had gotten herself lost in the unfamiliar woods. She stood still to listen for the wheezing sound of his sleeping breath, "Jake?" She whispered again.

"Hey." Finally a groggy voice floated through the trees towards her, she walked towards it relieved that she was not lost.

By the time she had reached their rocky hideaway Jake was up searching frantically through the brush. When he heard her approaching he jumped, looking at her with wide eyes, "Are you okay? I heard you calling." He clutched at his chest as though she had startled him, "I heard a loud noise. I thought you were hurt." He walked towards her with concern, approaching slowly as though he were afraid of spooking her. Jenny pointed to the forest behind her, looking carefully back to be sure nothing was behind her.

"Some sort of explosion, a little ways out. I don't know if it was a bad thing, or a good thing." She scrunched up her nose as she tried to decide which, "Someone could be looking for us." She shrugged hopefully and continued to stare at the trees warily.

In the distance the trees bowed and shook, as though some large creature was slowly making its way out towards them. Jake backed towards the rocks putting his arm between Jenny and the trees, "We should take cover, just in case." He waited for her to move as they backed slowly towards the rocks to hide.

Kneeling in the damp earth they peeked over at the malicious trees every now and again to be sure they were still safe. Jenny whispered to Jake after a few minutes had gone by with little commotion from the trees, "If it was help, do you think they would be louder?" She passed a quick glance towards the forest to be sure it stayed still, "Like, don't you think they would be calling? To see if anyone was out here?" Her brow furrowed at the thought of a large wild animal, about to lunge at them from within the trees.

Jake frowned as though he were considering the thought quite seriously, finally he turned his back to her, picking up a rock and a large stick. He pressed the rock into her palm and whispered back, "You're right."

Silence washed over them as the rustling grew louder. Jenny could hear voices in the trees, gruff and vaguely familiar but definitely human. She lowered the rock behind her back, just in case. She peeked out from her hiding spot, watching a shape come out from the woods. Dropping down from within the trees it stepped tentatively onto the rocks before calling back into the tree at someone else.

"The rocks should be safe." She could vaguely hear it calling. She looked at Jake with confusion, *why were the rocks safe?* And why was he climbing down from a tree? Jake raised an eyebrow as he raised a finger to his lips. Silently, Jake peeked around the rocks behind her, staring for a moment before leaping out from their rock hideaway.

"Bruce!" He called, running for the man who had just landed from within the tree. Jenny stayed hidden, clutching the rock as she waited to see what was happening.

Bruce looked up with relief and bewilderment as he landed on the rocky ground and saw his friend running towards him, "Jake, oh man we thought you were dead!" He pulled him in for a hug as relief washed over his worn face. Another figure stepped from behind Bruce. He was frowning, looking at Jake with a bit of contempt as though he had not found what he was looking for.

Jake watched him warily, wondering who he was. He held fast to the stick in his hand as he watched the man's features contort into a frown. Slowly he turned back to Bruce, beaming with relief.

"What on earth were you doing up a tree?" He asked slowly, watching the forest with concern.

"You wouldn't believe me if I told you." Bruce laughed shakily, wiping his face with his sleeve, "How on earth did you get all the way over here?" Bruce was looking past him now at the vast open sky beyond. He took a tentative step closer, peering awkwardly off the edge of the distant cliff.

"You wouldn't believe it Bruce, I had to climb up a rock wall that was at least twenty feet high..." Jake pointed back to where Bruce had been staring. Bruce took another step closer, looking down over the edge. He backed away quickly looking at Jake and shaking his head with a wild grin.

"That's crazy, how the heck did you manage that?" He asked, bemused.

Jake began to describe his journey to Bruce, relieved that his friend had made it out. He sat back on a rock to recount his heroic tale to Bruce while the other man paced at the forest's edge. He had seriously been starting to think he and Jenny were the only ones alive.

"We should head back." The other man said curtly as Jake was describing the rising tide. Bruce looked back with a nod.

"Yeah, soon." He nodded gruffly turning back to Jake to hear more.

Jenny watched from the bushes, watching Bruce's companion, with his familiar scowling face. He seemed more disappointed than he should have. She stared at him for another moment, wondering where Grace and Jerry were. Perhaps they hadn't made it through after all.

Finally she stepped forward to join the group and Ethan's face contorted into a beaming smile.

***

As Ethan stepped from the woods onto the rocks ahead, he felt relieved that he was finally safe from the woods. It would be very difficult to set up land mines in solid rock, so he knew they were past the danger zone, or at least that particular danger.

Ahead of him Bruce was talking to a young man, he had obviously found the person he was looking for. He seemed overwhelmed with joy, bantering about their travel to his friend. Asides from the single battered man, the area was clear, no chatter from other survivors. As the new man began to describe his ordeal and journey up the rock face, Ethan began to lose hope that Jenny had made it out at all. The surrounding silence seemed to reveal the fate of the others in the tail end of the plane. He had come this far for nothing, leaving Grace and Jerry in danger to chase after a ghost.

"We should head back." He suggested, defeated.

"Yeah, soon." Bruce waved a hand, turning back to his companion to hear more of his dramatic tale of survival. Ethan rolled his eyes, crossing his arms impatiently as he waited for the two to finish their chatter.

Then ahead, a figure stepped from behind some rocks, looking frazzled and dirty, probably as much as he did. It was Jenny.

She walked towards him with a worried smile, "Ethan?" She beamed, but her eyes remained vague, "Where is Grace?" She looked afraid to ask. He could see where she was coming from, he had emerged from the forest alone with a stranger and Grace was nowhere to be seen.

Ethan uncrossed his arms, taking a tentative step forward, he reached for her face, unsure if she was really standing there before him. She passed him a puzzled look.

"Where are Grace and Jerry?" She asked again, taking a step back as her face contorted with sadness.

"They're fine." He answered quietly.

"But, where are they?" She looked over his shoulder again, wondering if they were hiding in the forest.

"Grace and Jerry are on the beach with the others from the front of the plane." He explained. Suddenly her face opened up with a wide smile.

"Oh that's fantastic, are they okay then?" She didn't wait for an answer, pulling Ethan in for a wet muddy hug.

"Yes, yes, they were both alright." He strained to speak over her tight embrace.

"I was so worried!" Jenny cheered, squeezing him even harder. Ethan's back crackled in protest.

"We should get back to them. They were going to set a signal fire to call for help." Ethan gasped, finally freeing himself from her strangled embrace.

Bruce walked over, "This time let's take the beach. I don't want to get blown up in there." He jabbed a thumb towards the trees with a scowl.

"Blown up?" Jake asked with wide eyes, "Is *that* what the noise was?" He exchanged a look with Jenny, neither of them had even considered that the noise earlier had been an explosion near their friends. Jenny looked Ethan over for injuries, suddenly aware that he was covered head to foot in sticky dry blood. She touched his shoulder tentatively, searching for a wound.

"It's not mine." Ethan whispered, turning to Bruce so he could explain.

"Yeah and that's not the worst." Bruce began to walk in the direction of the beach, keeping a running banter about the adventure in the woods for Jake and Jenny to listen to. Ethan followed behind, diligently searching for oncoming threats as he scoured the tree line.

Somehow he didn't think the beach would be any safer.

SCAVENGE

Grace stood, staring towards the beach, with Jerry. In the breaking dawn, her survival instincts had kicked into full speed. Her brain raced with thoughts of Ethan and how he was faring on the other side of the island, how Jenny was, where Jenny was. She wanted to make sure help could find them. She was certain that someone was looking for them.

The sticky sand clung to her aching feet as she shuffled across the damp sand in front of Jerry. The tide had washed out, leaving in its wake debris from the wreckage that had stranded them. Grace had thought they would be safe by now. It seemed unusual to her that they hadn't heard any signs of planes or helicopters scouring the area. Her heart had sunken into a pit in her stomach. They were on their own.

If Colt was on the island or even controlling it from a distance they wouldn't stand a chance without back up. And all of the poor unwitting victims on the beach, she glanced back with sorrow. They hadn't a clue what they were up against. They didn't deserve this.

She walked up the beach to Jerry, watching his face as he stared out at the mess washing ashore. She wondered how he was doing, what he was thinking. He stared at the receding waves with a frown plastered across his worn face.

"Hey." She said softly, standing beside him to gaze out at the open water, hopeful that she would see a ship on the horizon.

"How much longer do you think they will be?" Jerry asked her suddenly.

Unsure if he was asking about Ethan or the rescue she responded, "I don't know."

"He should be back by now." Jerry mused. "Should we go look for him?"

She knew now that he was talking about Ethan, "It wouldn't do any good if we went and got ourselves lost in the woods." She said, knowing Ethan would want her to protest and keep Jerry on the beach. "They could be anywhere out there..." She continued with a little less enthusiasm.

Jerry shook his head, "That's what I'm worried about." He turned to look at the trees hopefully, "What if Ethan is lost?"

"He'll find a way. He always does." Grace placed her hand on Jerry's shoulder, noticing how damp and cold his shirt was under her fingers, "Jerry you're freezing!" She placed her other hand on his exposed arm, feeling the chill of his bare skin as she stared at him with worry.

"There's not much we can do about it, but wait for help, Grace." He turned back to her with a small chattering frown that she hadn't noticed before.

"We need to see if we can get some supplies out of the plane wreckage." She decided, walking towards the rubbish floating onto the beach. If they were lucky, some of the luggage might have something inside that they could use. Extra clothes or things they could burn in the fire to make the signal stronger and something to keep Jerry warm.

The others had begun working on the signal fire again, struggling to get the damp wood to light again from the embers of the fire they had managed to successfully ignite in the woods overnight. The only promise was the amount of smoke that the damp wood was sending into the air. If they could keep it up there might be hope.

As Grace reached the shore she steeled herself for the sight ahead of her. Several floating bodies mingled with the debris in the water, washing ashore as the tide went out slowly, leaving them stranded.

Her mouth felt dry as she passed by the forgotten passengers, she wondered if anyone from the upper beach was missing them. None had ventured back to the shore to search. It was probably better that way. The sight was gruesome, her breath caught in her throat at the smell. She forged through the cool waters to the first mound of luggage that she could see.

She pulled a heavy wet bag of luggage from the water, dragging it towards the dry sand before opening it. Water pooled out when she tugged the zipper open. As she flipped the lid open, clothes and personal things spilled forth with the rush of water. She rifled through the pile; nothing that could help them in their struggle for food and water. Still, she took some of the clothing and laid it out atop the luggage to dry, if they were here much longer it might be nice to stay warm.

Jerry was calling to her from the water edge, she raced to him. He was holding the handle of a yellow cooler and was dripping wet from his plunge into the waves.

"Jerry, you should stay up here and keep dry." Grace scolded him, helping him drag the container away from the lapping waves.

"It looks like it's from the airline." He ignored her, pointing to the writing on the side of the container. He was right, it had the airline emblem etched into the side of it which meant it was probably something they could use. She took a side of the cooler and helped him drag it up towards the luggage she had already pulled in. With a little fumbling, they managed to pry it open.

"Oh, perfect." Grace whispered. Inside were peanuts and mini bottles of water and liquor. It would help immensely. Pulling out two bottles and a couple of packets for Jerry, she closed it over.

"Stay here." She called back to Jerry as she began pulling it towards the fire where the rest of the crowd had gathered in their effort to signal for help.

She struggled with the weight of the container, dragging through the sand until someone noticed her. He raced down the beach to meet her, "Do you need some help?" He asked reaching for the handle. She nodded.

"We found some water and peanuts, take it up to them. I'll keep looking through the stuff in the water." She let go of the handle so he could take over.

"That's great, thanks." He nodded to her as he began to pull the cooler away. Grace walked back to Jerry at the water. He was waiting for her, holding the two bottles she had tossed into the sand before trekking up the beach.

"Drink up." She called over the crashing waves when she got closer, waving ahead to encourage him to drink some water.

"Grace, I'm fine. Let's keep looking." He called back, placing the bottles in the sand by the other luggage for later, "I see more yellow over there." He pointed to a cresting wave. She looked towards it, seeing the yellow rolling in. It was the same color as the other cooler.

She waded out to see what might be in the other crate. The waves crashed against her knees, slamming debris against her shins and making her footing falter. Her shoes slid against the underwater rocks and she tripped, flailing as she crashed into the water heavily. Her tail bone struck against a rock sending a sharp pain up through her arms as she fought to right herself. Scrambling against slimy stones, she pulled herself upright, breath catching in her throat at the sudden deep chill of the water. She quickly scanned her surroundings, finding the beach again to catch her bearings.

Turning back to the waves, a chill rolled down her spine as the parcel splashed against her fingertips and she was able to hook it and bring it in towards her. It was heavier than the other cooler, and sloshed like it had been filled with water. She pulled it through the waves towards the shore, holding on tightly as it tried to slip away from her with every wave. She tugged at it when it stopped floating and began to pull on the bottom. When she had made it to the beach Jerry was waiting to help her drag it through the sand.

Jerry helped her unclasp the sides when it was settled in the sand. She pulled back the lid, holding her breath, she peered inside.

"Finally." She whispered, staring at the contents in awe.

PROGRESS

Ethan was falling behind again. His efforts to keep watch of the tree line set him a full four paces behind the others. The lumpy rock riddled sand turned his ankles painfully as he walked; he was too busy watching the surrounding area for threats to care.

The beach was damp from the receding tide, they stuck close to the lapping waves hopeful that any dangers would have been swept away with the tide. It made walking much more tedious as they struggled through debris and sand covered rocks, upset their footing, but Ethan felt a little safer knowing that Jenny was less likely to set off a land mine or be ravaged by a wild beast. Grace would be upset with him if he lost her on the way back after all the effort he had gone through to find her in the first place.

Bruce was chatting away in front of him with Jake and Jenny. They were exchanging stories about the crash and the aftermath. Ethan was only half listening, it sounded like Jake and Jenny were the only ones to escape the back of the plane as it had disappeared. He bit his tongue as he wondered what they would tell the others when they reached the beach, it wasn't good news for most of them.

Falling farther behind, he tuned them out. He listened to the crashing waves at his feet while he watched the tree line grow farther away, giving way to a wider expanse of beach. He had been scanning the border between the trees and the beach cautiously while he walked, wondering when the next disaster would strike, until he finally saw something worth noting. A small transformer tucked behind the tree line drew him closer. He paused in the wet sand, standing still as he scanned the trees surrounding it.

With a start, he began running as best as he could on the slippery wet beach, towards Jenny and the other two, chatting while they walked. When he was close enough to hear them over the roar of the water he called ahead.

"Jenny!" He shouted, waving his arms when she turned so he would catch her attention. The others followed her while she walked back to him. "Look at that, a transformer." He pointed to the tree. By now Jenny and Jake had been caught up with the trials that had occurred in the woods on their way to find the survivors from the tail end of the plane. They both looked at the forest with wonder.

Ethan had pulled Jenny aside earlier, tentatively explaining the flaming letters on the forest floor. She had agreed that it smelled suspiciously like Colt was involved somehow. They had agreed that they would need a way to signal for help and get the attention of King and Chung, who had probably not sent them onto the plane in the first place. Jenny was playing the news close to her chest, afraid of the other two getting caught up in the chaos.

Ethan had wanted to tell them, for their safety, but Jenny had pleaded with him to keep it under wraps, at least until she knew them better. Ethan wondered what more she needed to know, did she suspect that Jake was working with Colt? Or was she just afraid of making things worse?

Ethan had agreed to keep quiet until she was ready to let them in.

Maybe it was better that way, telling them who they really were could put their new companions in danger if Colt were to find out and target them. It could throw their lives into ruin, as it had done for Jenny and Ethan. That was the last thing he wanted to do to another person. He knew how it felt to be trapped in a safe house, wondering if he was really safe and when he would get his freedom and his life back.

Shaking the thought aside, Ethan looked up. The others had joined him on the shore, staring at the spectacle in awe as they contemplated what to do with the new information. Slowly and carefully they walked across the widening beach to get a better look at the sight before them. The slow static buzz of the transformer greeted them when they drew closer, leaving the lapping waves in the background.

"It's live..." Jake said, listening close to the hum of the transformer overhead. He took a tentative step closer, looking up to see it better. Something overhead shifted and caught his eye, "It looks like there's a small wind turbine generating the power." He pointed overhead at the slow spinning spire as it poked out from behind the trees. It appeared to be in the distance, which meant there would have to be a clearing near the center of the island. Jake looked to Bruce, with fire in his eyes.

"Should we?" He asked his friend quietly, rubbing his hands together with a smirk.

"I bet if we followed the wires it would lead us to the psycho that set those land mines..." Bruce was only half serious. But if he ever saw that guy he was ready to rip him a new one. Ethan covered his face, concealing the small smile that had escaped at Bruce's comment, if only he knew how psychotic their foe really was.

"You know," Jake stepped forward thoughtfully, "We probably should find the guy. I mean, when help does come they'll want to get him for what he did to us..."

"I really would like to slap... that guy," Jenny added after a long stare into the trees, passing a glance towards Ethan. It seemed that Bruce and Jake had come to the conclusion that their elusive foe was still on the island. Jenny shared a look with Ethan, knowing that they didn't need to share the rest of the details just yet.

"Then it's decided," Bruce announced, he started towards the transformer cautiously, "Watch your footing and keep a good space... just in case." His bravery wavered as he waited for someone else to take the lead. Instead they fell in line behind him, leaving a four foot gap, in case of explosion.

Jenny and Jake were wary of following Bruce into the woods after hearing of their earlier ordeal with the explosives. Jenny scanned the forest floor before each cautious step, placing her feet with uncertainty as she scanned ahead into the rest of the forest.

Ethan watched as they began their detour through the forest, realizing after a few moments of tentative stepping that Colt would have to be a moron to put land mines or dangers anywhere near the wire from the transformer. He would risk cutting his own power supply if something were to detonate. He kept his mouth shut as he watched the others cautiously taking steps forward, at least they were alert for any other danger the forest held.

The wires ran overhead but below the treetops. It was easy enough to follow if they watched the black coiling cords. It didn't stay in a straight line, winding them through the trees as it looped about, soon leaving them unsure which way the beach had gone. Whoever owned the island had obviously not wanted to intrude upon nature too much when building whatever homestead they were obviously in search of.

Ethan watched overhead as the black cables took another strange turn around a large tree, Bruce had already veered to the left to follow it.

The woods were quite thick in this part. He waited tentatively to be sure Jenny made it around the low branches alright, she was being awfully quiet.

Soon the two had caught up, "Remember what Bruce said," Ethan warned, interrupting their chat, "keep your eyes open." He nodded his head meaningfully towards Jenny before walking onward into the woods. She stared back at him, suddenly scanning the surrounding forest while she walked.

Some sections of the forest looked more worn than others as though they were walking over a natural path that led through the thick forest. It appeared to lead somewhere, cutting though the path of the wire more than once. But they were reluctant to leave the wires, worried of becoming lost when they already knew the woods were dangerous. So they continued to follow the wires, using them as a guide.

The pace was slow, they combated fatigue and hunger with the overwhelming thirst that came from not having a drop to drink in nearly twenty-four hours. Jenny was exhausted, trying to keep her eyes open, she fumbled over a tree root. She could see Jake fighting through the brush ahead of her. After Ethan's reminder the two had split up. He had insisted on walking in front, so she would be the last to reach any danger. In her mind she was now the most likely to get picked off.

Jake seemed nice enough though and he had his heart in the right place. She was glad his friend had made it out alive. They had been on their way to Bruce's wedding, flying in ahead of the others so Bruce could pick up the decorations a day early. Jake had been his best man. Jenny really felt bad for the two of them, stuck on this island instead of preparing for the wedding and all because some crazy person had it out for Grace and Ethan.

They still had time though; as long as help came soon, Bruce and Jake would make it to that wedding. Jenny just hoped she could keep them in one piece. She had grown sort of fond of Jake and his chivalry through their trials. She didn't know if she would have fought so hard to make it if he hadn't been there to encourage her. She had reached the island in a depression, believing that they were the only survivors, she had not had much fight left in her. Now she was relieved that she had pushed through; looking forward to her reunion with Grace and Jerry and returning to her life in the real world.

The path became swampy ahead, Bruce slowed as bugs fluttered around them in swarms and thick muck crawled through their shoes and up their calves. The air was dense with humidity and smelled of moss and rotting wood. Jenny covered her nose when she grew closer, the scent made her empty stomach churn. She watched Bruce trudge forward, losing more and more of his foot to the slimy muck beneath his feet. It slowed his progress as it began to crawl above his knees.

"This isn't quicksand, is it?" Jenny called forward when it began to slither up to her ankles. Her shoe made a sucking sound as she tried to pull it back up. It was stuck, she leaned over to loosen it.

"No, just some lowland, there must be water nearby," Jake called back over his shoulder as he trudged on through the mess, "We might be able to find some fresh water though, if we find the source." He sounded hopeful and as thirsty as the rest of them.

"Water?" Bruce called back to him, "You think there'll be drinkable water around here?" He laughed, squelching farther through the muddy pit.

"There's gotta be a well or something, if they've got electricity, then they have water..." Ethan chimed in, wanting to get his two cents in before the other two men started bickering again.

Suddenly Jenny was thirsty again, she had gotten into a rhythm of steps pushing the thought of food and water out of her mind as she trudged through the thick mud concentrating on keeping her shoes intact. The mention of water left her dry mouth fighting to drool at the thought.

Jenny kept that thought in her head, fresh water nearby. She pulled herself through the mud, with high hopes of being rewarded with a cool drink. Even a not cool drink would be nice right about now. She had probably sweated out most of the fluid in her body. Her head was aching, she squinted forward to oppress the blurring of her vision. She wasn't sure how much more she had in her to keep going forward. She wouldn't survive if she gave up now, but she wasn't sure she would do much better if she kept up without some sustenance.

Bruce had stopped ahead, waiting for them to catch up to him in the small clearing he had found. Ethan struggled to make his way over the last of the fallen logs and onto solid ground before Bruce uncovered his big discovery.

"Look... a well." He smiled at Ethan, pointing beside them to a small stone circle in the clearing.

It sat in the center of the small area, Ethan could almost imagine a beam of sunlight breaking through the upper foliage to surround the small well. It seemed like a miracle that they had happened upon; a source for fresh water after so much turmoil. Ethan wasn't about to look the gift-horse in the mouth now. Instead he stood with Bruce at the edge of the clearing waiting for Jenny and Jake to catch up so they could share their first drink of water since the accident and perhaps take a moment to enjoy it before confronting the thing that awaited them at the end of the black coil overhead.

Finally Jake broke free of the mud, turning back to give Jenny a hand over the last hurdle, when he turned around his jaw dropped.

"You were right man," Bruce gave him a pat on the back, "Fresh water for all."

Jake smiled, "What are we waiting for?" He cheered, about to take a step forward into the clearing.

"Hey, remember what happened to us in the forest?" Bruce cautioned, pointing to Ethan for a reminder, "Take it easy."

Ethan took the lead, he made his way over cautiously, startling easily at the snapping of twigs underfoot. Behind him, Jake and Jenny were trying to follow his footsteps with care.

The well was clean and appeared to be maintained and used regularly. It brought more belief to the idea that someone had a cabin on this island. It was habituated, at least some of the time. Beside the well was a small pump, presumably for the ease of accessibility. Ethan approached it cautiously as Bruce stood back to scan the area for threats. As Ethan reached for the handle he noticed a small clear thread attached to the handle. Cautiously he touched the thread, running his hand upwards towards the trees. He stopped following the wire when it reached too high and became invisible among the trees. It looked suspicious, though he couldn't imagine the purpose. He walked back to the pump, watching the woods as he gave it one tentative push.

Immediately something snapped in the woods, cracking above his head, "Hit the ground!" He yelled into the silence as he dove at the ground, pressing his face into the damp earth while he covered his head.

"Argh!" Jake screamed behind Ethan, he heard two muffled thumps and the twang of a chord being let go.

Ethan turned over, staying on the ground as he scanned for Jenny, "Jenny are you alright?" He called across to her once he had seen her laying on the ground across the way.

"Yeah," she called back, "what was that?"

"I don't know, something was attached to the pump."

"It was an arrow." Jake called angrily from behind Jenny. Slowly he got up to his knees, holding his shoulder tenderly as blood trickled down his shirt to his waist.

"Are you alright?" Bruce asked, jumping up and racing across the clearing to check his friend over. Jake stayed where he was, sitting back onto the wet ground with a gasp as his shoulder shifted.

Ethan made his way over slowly, reaching him at the same time as Bruce. He reached out to touch the arrow protruding from Jake's shoulder, it stuck out the back of him like a branch on a tree. Around him a scattering of arrows had stuck into the ground. Ethan ripped off a piece of his tattered shirt, slowly making strips of dirty fabric as Jake closed his eyes.

"How bad is it?" Jake finally asked, unsure if the silence was their way of mourning a loss. "Is it bad?" He asked again when no one answered.

"You're gonna have to leave it in." Jenny finally replied, distracted as she thought of how to stop the bleeding. She knew taking the arrow out would only cause more blood and they couldn't guarantee that it hadn't splintered inside his shoulder. It was a miracle that it had only gone in as far as it had, as Jenny looked closer she realized it had probably struck his bone and gotten stuck. She winced at the thought, looking up towards the treetops to see where the shot had come from.

"We need water." Bruce announced as he observed Ethan making strips out of a section of shirt, "To drink, and it would help if we could soak some of those." He pointed to Ethan's handiwork.

"How do we get water without triggering something else?" Jenny asked, still scanning the trees.

"Maybe if we cut the line it'll stop it from triggering." Bruce walked to the well to have a look at the line attached to the pump. He followed it by sight, afraid to touch the string for fear it would send another spray of arrows their way. "Can you guys clear out so I can cut this?" He finally asked, realizing that without any tools he was going to have to yank the string to free the pump for them.

"Yeah, give us a minute." Jenny replied, kneeling beside Jake to help him right himself. "Careful now." She cautioned as she and Ethan helped him rise from the ground. The movement caused more blood to drip from his wound. He winced, holding his shoulder while he tried to catch his feet beneath him.

Slowly they moved him towards Bruce, tucking into a set of thick bushes behind their brave companion so he could release the tripwire.

Bruce stood diligently by the post waiting until his comrades were clear of the obvious line of fire before he began to untangle the tripwire. The wire was clear and appeared to be a thick fishing wire in its clear and strong nature. He looked around the area for something to aid his struggle with the wire, hoping to find a sharpened rock or something that could break through it without triggering it again. Finally he gave up his search, lifting his foot he struck down at the tripwire, knowing it would go off again, he only hoped he used enough force to sever it at the same time.

There came a sharp twang overhead and the scattering of arrows as they struck the clearing and stuck in the muck or pinged against the rocks. He ducked behind the small pump, hoping it provided him some coverage as the others hid in the bushes.

After a moment of silence he looked up. It had worked, the tripwire had been dislodged from the pump handle, "All clear." He called to the others.

"Did it work?" Jake asked groggily, peeking his head from behind the bush.

"Yep, we should be able to use it now." Bruce replied as he walked towards Jake to help him out of the tangling brambles.

With a few scrapes and bumps they made their way out and towards the pump, collapsing heavily on the ground before the well. Excitement washed over their tired faces as they anticipated the cool water they were about to enjoy.

They took turns handling the pump as they drank in the tangy water, uncaring if it was purified or in a fancy bottle, it was delicious to their parched mouths. It tasted earthy and metallic against Ethan's dry lips, he could feel his stomach sloshing as it filled. He had never been so grateful for a rusty pump in his life.

They sat at the well with satisfaction when they had drunk all the water their bodies could carry, their stomachs easily upset after the large amounts they had had. They took some time to dampen the cloth Ethan had prepared, dressing Jake's wound as well as they could to staunch the bleeding until they could get him medical attention and remove the arrow safely. It seemed to work, he carried his arm in a sling made of shirt fabric nodding that he would be alright to go on. Though they all knew he would need to be looked at sooner than later, or risk a serious infection.

Soon they would have to continue on, the cabin would be near and that would be where Colt would have himself holed up, watching their every move.

Ethan was ready.

SIGNAL

Grace rejoiced as she pulled the plastic packaging from inside the water filled cooler, so thankful that they had been double wrapped against water and humidity. She raced across the beach towards the crowd, leaving Jerry behind in her haste.

She ran to talk to Jarred, who had taken charge of lighting the fire. He seemed to be the undeclared leader of the beached party. He stood at the edge of the smoldering mound with his hand at his chin, watching the smoke curl up with thought. He turned when he saw Grace running up the beach towards him, taking a step towards her as he watched.

"I found flares!" She shouted when she got near enough for him to hear. Jerry followed slowly behind her, trudging through the sand with effort, "I have flares!!" She shouted again, waiving the bag as Jarred and some of the others looked her way.

Jarred froze for a moment as he processed her words, then he took off racing down the beach to meet her with excitement.

"Flares?" He asked as he drew near, his smile beamed with elation. "How many?" He asked peeking around her arm at the bag she was holding. She shook the bag in front of her, showing him three.

"Great, we can signal for help and start the fire, that way when the flare dies out we'll still have the smoke signal." He helped her peel open the packaging, "You do the flare, I'll start the fire?" She nodded in agreement, turning her back to the crowd. She was glad that he had a plan.

"I'll take it to the shore." She nodded to him again, walking towards the waves as he took the rest of the bag back to the pile of smoldering wood.

"Thanks." He called as she retreated back towards Jerry.

She met Jerry halfway to the shore. He had taken a pause on the beach, catching his breath in heaving gasps. By the time he had righted himself Grace was already standing before him.

"How many were there?" He asked as Grace approached him, turning to join her on her walk to the waves.

"Three." She replied waiving the one in her hand triumphantly. "They are going to use one to light the fire, want to help me set this one off?" She watched his tired face with anticipation, she was nervous that she would mess it up somehow, never having set off a flare before.

"Of course." He smiled back, patting her on the shoulder. Grace reached for him, looping her arm through his elbow to assist him down the beach with ease.

He wanted to tell her he was alright, that he could do it on his own, but the strain of the last day was wearing on him and he appreciated her concern. He patted her hand, nodding up towards her with a smile, wondering what he would do without her. Slowly they trudged back down the beach, tired from their race up through the sand to deliver the flares to Jarred.

When they reached the shore Grace sat on the sand, helping Jerry sit next to her on the beach while she dug out a small hole to pace the flare in. She looked over the packaging for a moment, passing it to Jerry in hopes that he could decipher the small diagrams better than she.

Finally when they had decoded the tiny message she pulled the cap off of the tube revealing a small black flare. She struck it against the cap after reading the instructions on the side of the tube for a third time to be sure. It lit at the end. She frowned as she placed it into the sand to secure it.

"Not really what I was expecting." She turned to Jerry with a frown, "Shouldn't there be fireworks or something?"

He laughed, "It's a flare Grace, not a firework. If someone flies overhead, they might see it, and then the smoke from the fire will alert them that we need help."

"Oh." She answered softly, watching as a few spikes of fire flew overhead leaving a trailing snake of smoke wafting towards her face. Soon it had died to a small simmer at their feet.

She looked back to the fire, hoping it would get started soon, or at least give them some smoke to work with, "I was hoping it would be more, I thought it might help Ethan find us too." She was frowning now, worried about his progress. What had he found on the other side of the island? Had he even gotten there? And what of Jenny? She stood slowly, moving to where Jerry was sitting on the other side of the flare. She sat back next to him, leaning on his shoulder for comfort. "I hope they are okay." She whispered.

"Me too." He agreed, watching the water rolling in towards their toes.

***

Chung was ready to throw in the towel, or steal the boat. Unfortunately he didn't know how to drive a speedboat and he needed to get to the real wreckage, which was nowhere to be seen. He turned to the captain.

"This isn't the wreckage, it's obviously been drifting. There are no bodies. Where are they?" He was losing patience with the coast guard and their inability to stray from protocols. At this rate he wasn't sure how Jenny would be when they *did* find her. Still his mind was spinning him between the best and worst scenario as he thought of her. Had they made it out safely, waiting for rescue on a yellow raft somewhere? Or was she beneath the waves, lost forever?

King was pacing again, looking over the debris they had pulled up as though it were a rummage sale. He sifted through the objects distractedly turning over one item after another as though he were looking for something in particular. A frown wore through his weathered face as he picked up a wallet, sifting through the contents with curiosity. He tossed it back onto the pile with distaste as he made his way back to the crew to help them bring more in debris.

As dawn broke, the spotlights became a blaring obstacle, reflecting off of the water and into their eyes. Soon they took pause to put them away while they took another trip to the docks to unload. King was exhausted as he stood on the crowded dock waiting for the all clear to board again. Chung stood silently beside him, rage radiated from his prone form as he fumed at the thought of another delay.

"This is just wrong." He declared, breaking his silence, he turned to confront King, the only person who would listen to his ranting.

"I know," King agreed slowly turning to his partner as his aching muscles protested the movement. "I haven't found anything of theirs yet..." He trailed off, referring to his search through the debris on board.

"That doesn't mean one of the other boats hasn't." Chung turned sharply, aborting their conversation as the call came to board the boat again.

The ride back to the site was silent as Chung stood in the center of the vessel, radiating a vibe that left the crew mute in its wake.

King reached for a pair of binoculars from within his vest. He stood tall at the stern of the vessel, scanning the horizon for any sign of life elsewhere. They all knew that the rest of the bodies weren't at the site, they had to be somewhere. His tired eyes grew weary as the rocking of the waves made his steady hand falter, but there was nothing else he could think of to get this mission going faster than finding a new direction himself.

Shortly the captain joined him, "Any luck sir?" He asked pulling forth a second pair of binoculars.

King shook his head. "Nothing, just more water." He pointed towards the middle of the vast Gulf. "What's that fuzzy thing out there?"

The captain took the binoculars in his hand to his eyes, scanning the area King had pointed to. "It looks like smoke, could be a low cloud or a storm. We could go closer to have a look. I think there is an island out that way." He nodded to King as he pulled back from the perch where they stood, pulling the ropes and lines in. Finally they were getting somewhere.

Before pulling away from the site he called over his radio, "This is boat alpha, heading out to look at an anomaly on the horizon, over." He waited for the others to respond with acknowledgment before he put the boat into drive, slowly weaving through the debris towards the horizon.

Chung had snapped his head up at the mention of smoke, suddenly the fury he had been emitting had changed. The crew could feel it, resuming their regular chatter as Chung's watchful eyes were put to better use watching the horizon.

Chung snatched the binoculars from King, observing ahead as they approached, "It's smoke," he called to the captain over his shoulder as he watched with thoughtful attention, "It looks like a signal fire." He confirmed as he tried to get closer or higher up to get a better look. The sway of the boat prevented him from standing as tall as he would like. He grasped for a railing as a heavy sway sent him teetering towards the froth below. "Get us closer." He demanded, finally feeling a small ray of hope that his sister might still be out there.

King pulled the binoculars back into his hand, "Find your own." He huffed, looking towards the area himself, craning his neck to see the smoke. He observed a small spiral of hazy dark smoke curling up into the sky before dissipating in the breeze, a strong sign that it was indeed smoke from a fire. The fire itself could be from anything, there was no guarantee that it was intended as a signal. It could be someone trying to clear away some brush on the island by burning it away, likely it was not accidental.

The captain approached King, pulling his own binoculars to his eyes for a better look. He stared towards the presumed smoke signal with concern, "There is an island out there. It's private, but I haven't seen anyone out there in ages and no boats have left the dock towards it recently."

He quickly pulled up his radio, turning his back on King as he headed towards the crew. The muffled exchange on the radio was too quiet for King to overhear, he suspected that the captain had retreated so he couldn't interfere. They were bringing the rest of the boats. After a few more communications between the intercoms he turned to face King, "Hold on boys," he called to the two agents, "We're going in."

***

Jenny was beyond tired, her muscles ached in places she had never felt before. She stood, grinding her teeth as she shook off the desire to curl up and sleep after filling her belly with water.

"We should keep going, the cabin should be close." She suggested, rousing the others from their satisfied stupor.

"Yeah, we should go check that out." Bruce agreed, holding a hand out for Jake as he stood slowly, stretching out his neck with a loud crack.

"Thanks," Jake said, taking Bruce's hand to help him upright. He adjusted the splint on his arm with care, looking overhead to find the wires they had followed in. "That way." He declared, pointing to the trees where the black cables wound back out of the clearing into the woods.

Ethan took the lead again, watching overhead as the black cables led him forward.

TROUBLE

The girl was right, the well was close to the cabin. As they gathered themselves and prepared to continue on he was watching them from a camera, amused and enthralled that he finally had visitors. Suddenly a surge of adrenaline raced through his veins as he anticipated the rush of meeting them.

He hadn't expected them to come looking for him, it was a welcome surprise. He stood formally, imagining the greeting he would welcome them with, the stature he would hold, the weapon he would choose.

Slowly he paced the small cabin, watching his monitors with excitement while he waited. The plane crash had taken its toll on him as well. A spike of pain in his shin told him he had been injured when he had ejected himself from the plane. But he would still be able to pick them off, one at a time.

Until no one was left to stand in his way.

He watched on the screens as they struggled through the bushes, chuckling that they had no knowledge of the pathway on the other side of the well, it would have taken them straight to the front door. Instead they had been set wandering slowly in the woods, weaving their way to him, camera to camera. On the upside, if they were following the wires, he would be able to see them the whole time.

He switched over his screens, focusing on the beach for a moment while he listened to the microphones surrounding the wanders in the woods. Things were shaping up just as he had planned. He turned two of the screens back to the woods, watching as they approached. One of them had been injured by his trigger at the well. Something he hadn't anticipated being much use, funny how he had been standing in just the right spot and not at the well when it had happened. *Pity it hadn't been Ethan*, he thought.

The circuitry of the cameras had been in place when he had commandeered the island several years ago after the previous owner had been incarcerated, with much credit to his own meddling. Not many others knew of the islands whereabouts, which is what made it so perfect. He had wanted to find the perfect location, desolate and hard to find help. The island had been absolutely perfect for his purpose.

He had stayed on the island alone for months, learning the layout of the land as he prepared. The additional cameras and unexpected surprises had been his own final touches on his masterpiece. Then it had laid in waiting for this moment, the day when he would wipe the entire Evans' line from the face of the earth, Grace included. And that gossip of a butler, he was more their family now than he had been when Mr. Evans had been captured.

It infuriated him, how that one man had kept them all together. Ethan should have fallen apart when he had lost his best friend and his father, instead he had found a reason to thrive. That damned old man would pay like the rest of them.

Taking care of the bedridden Mr. Evans back on the main land, would be a walk in the park. He had been monitoring the patient closely.

Mr. Evans was unlikely to ever wake from his coma, with much thanks to the secret doses he had administered while visiting. Soon it would all be over and then he would have his throne. No one would question his ability to execute a job, no one would presume he was riding the coat tails of the Great Hart. Hart's family was his first act of treachery, all his own.

Cutting his ties to Hart was his beginning.

***

Grace stared back to the roaring fire, briefly excited that it had finally started smoking enough to signal for help. She turned back to the shoreline, watching the horizon with anticipation. How long would it take to catch someone's attention, she wondered.

Jerry had fallen asleep lightly beside her on the sand using some drying luggage to rest his head. His breathing was heavy and labored. Grace was worried about him. At his age an excursion like this could be extremely dangerous to his health.

Behind her she heard screams, checking Jerry over one last time she tossed an extra shirt over his arms, protecting him from the sun before she ventured up to the others to see what the commotion was about.

Grace traced her way through the sand to the fire, listening intently for the sound that had piqued her curiosity. The chatter around the fire was minimal. Most that were there were resting in hopes of being rescued soon. Others were out foraging the shoreline like she had for supplies, some were in the woods looking for food. Many of the passengers had become sick from the heat and extreme of their peril. They had taken to heaving into the brush behind the fire. The strain of the journey was finally taking its toll as the adrenalin wore off.

She stood silently waiting for the scream to begin again, it hadn't come from the fire, she had been too far away to pinpoint exactly where. Someone was probably lost in the woods, having strayed too far to find privacy again. The crackle of the fire was loud beside her, she stepped away towards the woods to hear clearer. Soon she heard it again, strangled and desperate. The screaming came from the woods beyond their tree shelter. She ventured out slowly, cautious of the surrounding environment. It sounded like a man, yelling for help. As she drew neared she tried to pinpoint the source.

"Hello?" She called before her cautiously.

"Help!" Came the long moaning call somewhere ahead of her, she peered forward into the bushes.

"Where are you?" She paused, standing still for a moment, afraid of falling for a trap.

"I fell in a hole, its Jarred." The voice came slower, breathing heavily with pain.

Grace hadn't seen Jarred out at the fire, at the time she assumed he was taking a washroom break or finding more wood. Grace cautiously walked forward, wary that the hole that Jarred had fallen into was somewhere ahead of her. Finally she saw it. A scattering of sticks lay around the edge of the large crater. He had obviously been looking for more wood for the fire when he had fallen in. Grace peered down.

The hole was nearly ten feet deep, water pooled at the base around Jarred's tangled body. He was surrounded by the remnants of the covering that had fooled him into falling. Sticks and leaves scattered about him, clinging to the walls as they continued to fall. He had fallen recently. A thin covering of twigs and leaves had covered the entrance, much like the small traps children set for their friends as a joke. Although this seemed much more dangerous and purposeful. Grace looked about the area with suspicion.

Jarred looked hurt, he had settled into an awkward position that looked unnatural to Grace. He held his head above the water with effort.

Grace could see his strain as he looked up at her pleadingly.

"I'll need to get help to pull you out of there." She called down to him, "Hold on Jarred, I'll get some help." She paced hastily back through the woods being as careful of her own footfall as she could.

"Help!" She called when she reached the small group huddling around the fire, slowly they turned to see who was calling. The crowd slowly drew closer so they could see what was wrong. "Jarred fell in a hole, I need help to get him out." She said when they had quieted to listen to her.

One of the men stepped away from the group, approaching Grace.

"Is he okay?" He asked leading her back towards the woods. He stopped, allowing her to take the lead so she could show him where Jarred was.

"No, he's hurt, it's a pretty deep hole. I'm going to need some help getting him out." She scoured the area for something that might help retrieve him from the bottom as she took the lead to show him the way. She pointed into the woods to where she could hear Jarred's labored breathing, wheezing out of the hole and drifting through the woods to them. "He's out that way," she told him, picking up some sticks in case they needed them for a tourniquet or something, "be careful, watch where you step."

She still wasn't sure how they would get him out. It was a deep hole and he appeared to be in no condition to climb, but she felt guilty leaving him on his own and injured. So she didn't want to waste time making a plan, she was in a hurry to make it back to his side, even if only for the moral support.

"Hang on." The man called to her as he stopped and turned to race back to the beach. Grace stood in the woods alone for a moment wondering what idea he could have had. He returned a moment later with an armful of the clothing they had retrieved from some of the suitcases. He obviously had a plan. With a grim smile of appreciation, Grace led the way back to the hole careful of her footfalls for fear of other dangers.

The hole was easier to locate this time around. She saw the branches piled at the edge and knew not to go any farther into the small clearing. Slowly she tip toed around it with the man following close behind her, clinging onto the clothing in his arms so he didn't drop them into the gaping hole.

"I'm back." Grace called down, scanning the hole for Jarred. The sun had tucked itself behind a cloud making the opening dark, she could make out a faint outline as he tried to move above the water pooling around his body.

He garbled speechlessly from the bottom, echoing upwards with appreciation. Grace retreated back over the side of the hole to see what the plan was. Her new companion was surveying the scene silently, looking up for tree branches they could use in their favor. Still scanning, he dropped the bundle of clothing to the ground and turned to Grace.

"I think our best bet is some sort of rope," he pointed overhead at a thick branch, "we can wind it over that to make it lighter to pull." He commented as he pulled a pair of pants out of the pile at his feet. He began stretching them, tugging to be sure the material would hold. Grace picked up a shirt and a sweater, getting to work on knotting them together.

Grace's new comrade seemed poorly equipped to be tying a secure knot rope, she glanced over to see him struggling valiantly with a pair of pants as he failed to securely intertwine them with a shirt.

"Here," she said, taking the pile from his hands with a smile, "I'm quite good with knots." She commented, showing him how to twist the material together so the knots wouldn't slip.

He watched as she showed him on another section, nodding with approval as she demonstrated the strength, pulling the two ends to show

how it held together.

"That's much better." He agreed, taking one end of the rope and adding another shirt, testing his knots strength, he smiled.

Suddenly Grace felt like she could do this, she had practiced tying knots for years before her final escape from the tower, this felt familiar, she felt confident.

The material rope was almost complete when Jerry and a young woman emerged from the trees. Grace looked up with embarrassment, she had forgotten Jerry on the beach. Quickly she stood, calling to them across the gaping hole, "Watch out for the hole." Jerry looked startled. He stopped still and peered forward at the deep trench between them.

"What on earth is that doing there?" He asked with concern, looking at the rope Grace was making. "Is someone down there?" His eyes went wide as he finally saw the whole picture.

"It's Jarred, the fire guy. He was out getting more wood and he never came back." Grace's companion spoke up, nodding as he tied another knot.

"You shouldn't have wandered into the woods alone Grace." Jerry chided as he walked around the edge to join her.

"How can we help?" The young girl asked, staring into the hole as the sun peeked from behind a cloud. Her face contorted in horror when she finally saw Jarred in his predicament. "He's hurt." She announced, pointing to the hole as though it were something new.

"We know." The man beside Grace spoke quietly as he concentrated on a knot. The two of them had nearly finished making a rope to pull him out of the hole, taking turns talking aloud so he could hear their progress. He had quieted down, Grace peered back down at him. His labored breathing echoed up towards her, the only sign that he was still with them.

"We could use some help pulling him out." Grace smiled to the young girl. Her face had gone white at the sight of Jarred.

"Yeah, yeah, I can help pull..." She trailed off, taking a step away from the hole to lean on a tree. Grace could tell she was queasy from the sight, but any help was better than none at this point so she would accept the girl's offer.

Grace called down to Jarred while the other man finished tying the shirts together. She watched out of the corner of her eye, double checking his knots. She had once tied a rope out of sheets herself, she wanted to know that his work was secure and stable enough to pull Jarred up without hurting him more.

When the rope was done, he secured it around the base of a nearby tree before lopping it over the low branch and uncoiling it into the hole.

"Wrap it around yourself and hang on." He called down, making room for Grace to take hold of the shirts. Behind her Jerry and the young girl who had escorted him through the woods held tight.

"I got it." Jarred called back up feebly after a moment of struggle with the ropes. His breaths were drawn and raspy. Grace feared that it had already been too long, his injuries were untreatable on this island and they hadn't even had the chance to assess the extent. Even if they got him up and intact without breaking the rope, it would be a tiresome trek back to the beach. With his injuries he would need to be carried and Grace knew Jerry and the young girl wouldn't be much help with that.

"Ready, one two...three." They called in unison to him as they began to pull. The fabric stretched in their hands, warping as they pulled at it. He was heavy and Grace worried that some of the knots wouldn't hold on the fabric. She pulled harder, tugging with her whole body, hoping to get him out before the makeshift rope gave up on them. She dug her feet into the ground as they pulled him out, one shirt at a time.

They were starting to make good progress when a shirt caught on the branch they were using as a levy overhead. The stretch of the fabric was getting to be too much.

"Wait." Grace called ahead to the man at the front of their pulling line, "Hold it there, I have to get the shirt clear."

He dug his feet in as Grace let go of her position, racing to the trunk to climb up the low branch. With help from the others she managed to wiggle it free, jumping back down to resume the task of pulling Jarred back out, "Here we go." She yelled, giving the rope a good heave. Soon they were making progress again.

When Jarred had reached the top, he rolled over onto the dirt, gasping against the pain. Grace reached for him, holding him steady as she slowly helped him move away from the hole to assess his injuries.

A stick had pierced through his calf, protruding through the other side bloody and mangled. She left it there for fear of him bleeding worse. He held his arm close, he had probably broken it. She checked him over gingerly, afraid of hurting him more. He appeared as though he would be alright if they carried him. She looked to the man beside her with a frown.

"Help me carry him to the beach?" She asked hopeful that he would be willing. He was still panting from the exertion of pulling Jarred out of the hole. He smiled and nodded, taking the upper half of Jarred's body in his arms, he instructed Grace to prop his legs over her shoulders and lead the way.

She was careful picking up his injured leg, placing his knees above her shoulders so she would be less likely to touch the piece of wood protruding from his calf. He winced in protest as she gingerly placed her hands atop his knees to hold him in place. Behind her she could hear Jerry instructing the girl to help him collect the rest of the rope so they could bring it back to the beach.

Slowly she started forward, her legs buckling under the weight. She wove through the trees finding the widest path she could manage in the dense woods. At times she became entangled in the brush at her feet, struggling to free herself without being able to see down to her feet to aid her. She was slow moving under the weight and every time she heard him gasp she paused, afraid of causing him more pain.

Her back ached and she was slick with sweat as she trudged forward, listening intently to the woods around her. She tried desperately to see through Jarred's legs to the ground before her, wary of more traps or dangers. Her efforts were futile as she arched her back against the weight on her shoulders. Each step she took with caution, making the progress slow. It was a good thing he hadn't been too far into the woods when he had fallen, or she might not have been able to get him back out.

When they reached the beach, the others were waiting for him. They had made Jarred a soft bed out of clothing and luggage to comfort him while they waited for help. Grace smiled at their kindness as she helped him prop his leg up on a carry-on bag. Jerry untangled the coil of clothing beside her, passing it gently to another so they could use it to staunch the bleeding in Jarred's leg and better support his broken arm.

Now that he was settled on the beach in better light, it was more obvious that the arm he held to his chest was broken; swelling to twice its normal size it was apparent that the bones in his forearm were not aligned. His face was pale and sweaty under the dirt that had covered him in his exile. Soon his eyes were rolling back in his head as he failed to fight off the exhaustion that had surely overtaken him after his ordeal.

"Thanks miss." He whispered to Grace as his face went still. Grace stood watching him for a moment longer to be sure he was still breathing.

Taking Jerry's hand in hers, she nodded to the crowd that had gathered around Jarred, "Take care of him." She whispered as she turned to walk back to the water with Jerry. There was no more she could do for him now.

ENCOUNTER

Ethan had spotted the cabin. It lay in a clearing ahead. He and the others had stopped at the edge of the forest to make a plan. Inside, he and Jenny knew that a psychopathic killer awaited, ready to kill them all at the drop of a pin. Bruce and Jake were wary of the excursion, their bravery faltering as they reached the final destination.

As much as Bruce claimed he wanted to confront the person who had sabotaged the island for the unwitting survivors of a plane crash to succumb to, Ethan wasn't sure he had the courage to go through with it. Beside him, Jake was drawn and pensive, watching the cabin with suspicion as they waited.

Jenny and Ethan knew what the man behind the door was capable of doing to them. He feared that letting the others know the truth would set them running. His conscience was fighting itself in his head, he was leading them in blind, not allowing them to prepare like he and Jenny could. Unsure how much information he could trust the two with without putting himself and Jenny in more danger, he kept silent.

Ethan was terrified, adrenaline coursed through his veins as his heart pounded in his ears. He watched from the trees through the filthy cabin window for signs of movement or life, a flash of light within told him that Colt was there.

He was expecting them.

Around them the sound of electricity rang loudly over the silence of nature, flocks of birds flew away in fear and Ethan was prepared.

"Don't touch anything with metal on it, watch your step. He's set up an electric current somewhere, I can hear it." He announced to the others who were searching the forest for a source of the buzzing sound.

Jenny was slightly amused, "Is he running out of ideas or something?" She chuckled with excitement, she was going to get her revenge on this man for all that he had put her through and for her brother. "Well let's have at it." She continued, taking a thick stick from the forest floor for protection.

Bruce and Jake passed worried glances to one another at Jenny's reveal. Ethan shot her a look that she had said too much. She frowned, pursing her lips as she walked slowly towards the cabin. Ahead of her she could see a thin wire surrounding the place, it wound through the bushes and over the trees providing a protective barrier for the man inside. She swiped at the wire with the stick, jumping back as some of them bounced towards her on their downward journey.

"Come on guys." Jenny called back as she swiped again, batting the thread of wire out of her way as she closed in on the cabin. Nothing was going to get in her way, she was bound and determined. The metal hissed as it coiled towards her, sparks flying when the coil struck against itself. She threw herself back to avoid electrocution.

Ethan and Bruce took fallen branches from the ground and soon they were following her lead. They used the sticks to fold the wires away from the front doors so they could gain access to the cabin in the woods.

The snap and sizzle in the silence reminded Jenny and Ethan what they were up against. They couldn't take any chances here.

Something worse was waiting for them on the other side of that door.

**

King watched through the binoculars as they began their approach on the island. The small desolate place seemed to be a dot on the horizon, slowly growing as they approached. The thick smoke curled from the center of the shoreline, twisting lazily into the morning air. It was getting harder to see the haze as the smoke turned from the thick black that had lured them in to a soft white, barely visible unless you were looking for it.

The rest of the fleet had joined them. They had stopped at the docks to pack in more first aid supplies before catching up amid the swelling waves. King could see a tree line closing in on the horizon. Soon a rocky beach was visible as well.

The smoke was coming from the left side of the island, away from the visible dock. He could see small animated figures racing towards the dock, waving their tiny doll-like arms.

There were survivors.

They were closing in when something shot up from the islands interior. Like a missile, it came arching towards the waves in front of them. With a loud crash he was momentarily blinded as a flash through the binoculars scorched his eyes.

He dropped the binoculars, still fastened to his wrist as he blindly fumbled to catch hold of a railing to save himself from the sudden rough rocking of the vessel beneath his feet. He could hear the crew shouting over the ringing in his ears, just barely.

He blinked away the white dots that spotted his vision as he moved to get a better hold of the rail. Ahead of them something had exploded across the water. By the looks of it a slick of oil had lit up with a spark, billowing thick black smoke towards them. The flames licked at the hull dangerously close to their own fuel supply.

King gasped, breathing in the thick smoke as he tried to turn away. He looked across the smoky deck for Chung. Not seeing his partner, he began searching frantically until he spotted him, near the back, clinging to a rail as he heaved over the side. King smiled, Chung had only just kicked a stomach flu and boats were never his favorite.

"Hey!" King shouted over the uproar. Chung lifted his head heavily, looking towards King with concern.

"What on earth..." He began to retort when the captain turned, shouting commands to them over the chaos.

Sandbags and oars were tossed about. The crew began trying to keep the flames at bay while the captain amped up the speed to get them through the wall of fire. Swirling smoke billowed by them as they catapulted forward and lost sight of the other boats.

King and Chung held tight, holding their breaths as they passed through the thick dark haze. Flames licked momentarily at the side of the boat as the wake behind them sent the gas fire in all directions, spreading across the water in small fragmented patches.

Once they were past the smoke the captain slowed them, waiting for the other boats to make it through. The idling engine cut through the scattered cries on the other boats as they pressed through the wall of flames towards the island and the waiting fleet. Soon they had scattered the flames across the water and were waiting for the final command to approach the island.

King pulled the binoculars back to his eyes, scouring the now visible beach, counting the waiving bodies and searching for the faces he would recognize.

He saw her first, blowing red hair in a tangle, waving in the front of the crowd. Grace was on the island. They had found the survivors of the crash.

He waved Chung over, "I see Grace." He called through the chaos, Chung dashed across the deck, ripping the binoculars from King's arm vengefully. He held them up, scanning himself for Jenny. He walked across the deck for a better vantage point, ignoring the rest of the crew as he watched for Jenny to appear. She didn't appear to be on the beach with the others.

After a while he caught sight of Jerry, hanging in back by the trees. But Jenny was nowhere to be seen. His heart raced in his chest, breathing became difficult. He set his jaw and marched to the captain. "Get us to the island." He demanded.

The captain nodded grimly, knowing from the look on Chung's face that he hadn't found who he was looking for. He was not one to argue the value of family.

HOPE

Grace sat with Jerry on the shore waiting for the smoke signal to attract some attention. The flare had burnt out long ago, leaving a small ashen hole in the beach to mark her sitting place when she returned.

Jerry had enjoyed a nice nap on the beach, burning half of his face before going to meet Grace in the woods. The sting of the burn reminded him of their predicament every time he blinked.

Grace had apologized for not covering him over several times since and he had brushed it off, "No need to worry Grace." He had told her, gingerly feeling his face "How is the other gentleman fairing?" He asked after a period of silence. He had stayed back from the crowd once Jarred had been brought to the beach, knowing there was nothing he could do to help the situation. Jarred had seemed to be getting worse before Grace had left, blood was oozing from the stick in his leg and there was little they could do to stop the bleeding. He needed real medical attention.

"Not so good Jer, he needs real medicine and clean bandages...I don't think he'll get better on this island..." As she relayed the news to Jerry his sunburned face crinkled into a frown.

"We are going to need help soon..." He sighed, staring out at the water deep in thought. Grace wished she knew of another way to call for help. She wished their cell phones had been waterproof, but alas they had all died in the water and probably wouldn't have gotten a signal on the godforsaken island anyway.

Grace rose to stretch her legs, tossing a stone into the water with frustration, "Want to go for a walk along the shore and see if we can spot the others?" She asked tentatively, not really wanting to make Jerry exert himself too much. She was concerned with Jerry's deteriorating health. He seemed lethargic and unusually quiet as though he were in pain. Grace was aware that he should have been on some medications. She didn't know the full extent of his medical conditions. He had liked to keep that private.

With a small tired smile, he rose from the sand, brushing it off of his legs as best as he could, "Let's go see where they have gotten to." He agreed taking a careful step across the damp shore in the direction the tail end of the plane had washed away.

Really they had no idea where Ethan and the others had gotten to. They had chosen to take a route through the trees rather than staying on the shore to save time. Grace only had her own recollection of the direction in which the tail end had floated to give her a destination to search. She hoped that by walking down the shoreline they may be able to catch a glimpse of the small ragtag crew as they reached the other side of the island, perhaps a piece of the plane had washed ashore.

Ethan hadn't returned yet and she was becoming more and more worried. Just thinking of him set her heart racing with a fear that something was wrong. The thought that Colt might have sent them to the island only heightened her anxiety. Grace had heard noises from the woods on the other side of the island earlier in the morning. It had sounded like screaming.

She had wanted to run to Ethan then, to see if he was alright.

Instead she had focused on finding help, like he had asked. She wanted to believe that he could take care of himself and up until Jarred had fallen into that trap she had thought he would be alright.

After seeing what had happened to Jarred she had become concerned that the security cameras she had found were there to serve another purpose. Now she couldn't quell the idea that Ethan was in peril and though she didn't want to force Jerry to exert himself, she felt he would be safer with her.

Her nerves were wracked with feelings of guilt that she had let him go off alone with those strangers and feelings of remorse for those that hadn't made it to shore. When she closed her eyes she could hear the screaming and the crash of the plane hitting the water. She wouldn't be sleeping for a while. Jerry was hiding his worry much better, but she knew under his calm demeanor that he was just as concerned for Ethan's well-being. He moved quickly, holding out a hand to steady himself from the light-headedness that washed over him.

They had been walking for only a few moments when Grace noticed that Jerry was having trouble finding his footing in the thick damp sand of the shore. Waves lapped lazily about her feet, pushing more debris ashore as she turned to look at him closely.

"Are you sure?" She inquired again, wanting to continue, but not at the cost of her dear friend's health.

"Yes," he proclaimed, "perhaps we could find a source for water as well, I don't know if I can go much longer without." His voice was raspy, and Grace knew he was not one to complain, so if he was asking for water, he needed it badly.

"Good idea." She nodded, holding his hand. They started forward again.

The sand was thick with water from the receding tide and covered in a scattering of debris. Every footfall was made with much effort. Grace's legs had begun to ache from the exertion after only a few steps and Jerry was moving slower. She tried moving up the shore to the softer dryer sand but given their state of exhaustion it made little difference. Walking through the sand was a chore for them both.

Grace and Jerry had made it five minutes up the beach when she spotted a dock in the distance around the slight curve of the islands shore. It popped out towards the waves causing a disturbance in the tide that had drawn her eye to it, "Jerry, someone must live here, look there's a dock," she pointed with excitement, "maybe they have a well or something." She was smiling now, her over-exuberance extended to Jerry. He squeezed her hand with excitement, scanning the trees for a visible path to a homestead.

"Let's go have a look." He said, following her across the beach slowly to get a closer look at the area.

They were slow moving with Jerry's condition and their fatigue. Jerry was not use to physical exertion of this kind and his muscles ached without his arthritis medication. He bit his lip to cope with the pain in his joints and hoped it would all be over soon.

When they reached their destination a few grueling minutes later they were both slick with sweat and breathing heavily from the exertion. The dock protruded into the water six or seven feet. It looked old and neglected. The wood was warped and rotting through. There were holes in most of the graying wooden planks and it shook with each wave as though it were on its last leg. Grace had hoped to use the dock to check out the other side of the island. One disappointing look at the dock and she could tell it wouldn't hold her weight.

It gave Grace little hope that whomever owned the island visited often, or at all.

"I don't think anyone comes here anymore." She pointed this out to Jerry with disappointment. She frowned, turning to scan the trees for any other sign of life. Beyond the brush was a grown over pathway, if she tilted her head just right she could see where it had once been.

"It has most certainly not been visited for a long time," Jerry agreed, "perhaps it wouldn't be too smart to try and follow that, we might get lost. It looks grown over." He was not convinced they could find the path to follow, from their vantage point on the beach it looked overgrown. They were likely to get turned around and lost if they tried to follow it. There was no guarantee that it would even lead them to a well and after seeing the dock he doubted that the water supply would be in any better shape, even if they did find it. Suddenly he was thirstier than ever, knowing that their hopes of finding fresh water had been dashed so suddenly.

Jerry looked out to the water with disappointment. That was when he spotted something on the edge of the horizon, a small white dot hanging in peril between the water and the sky. He tugged Grace away from the forest by her forearm. She spun slowly, confused by his urgency.

"Look Grace," he raised an arm to point out past the dock, "is that a boat?"

Grace turned sharply, shielding her eyes against the sunlight glaring off of the water. She watched with anticipation as the small dot raced over the horizon so far away. "You're right Jer! Boats!" She yelled, dancing on the spot with excitement. "Do you think they will see us?" She asked with excitement when she realized there was more than one.

"Oh I hope so." Jerry said. He was shaking with anticipation, hopeful of being saved.

Soon there were more. They were small like tiny ants walking on the edge where the water met the sky, as they neared Grace could see that they were indeed boats. Her stomach churned with excitement at the prospect of help, or someone who could get them help. Grace waived her arms towards them, calling to the rest of those waiting on the beach.

"Guys!" She yelled as she waved her arms frantically, afraid to move from the dock in case she lost sight of the boats, "Boats!" She hollered louder. Soon they took notice of her frantic calling and began wandering over. When they saw the boats they started calling and waving their arms with her, trying to gain the boats' attention.

It didn't take long for the word to reach the rest of the survivors waiting on the beach. Soon they were adding more wood to fuel the fire, waving clouds of smoke out towards the water with fallen palm leaves. They were frantic to signal the boats in case they hadn't seen the small dots trying to wave them down from the dock.

Grace beamed as she became lost in the crowd. Help was on the way, finally. She thought of Jarred, needing medical attention so badly on the beach by the fire. Finally he would be able to get some real help.

Just as suddenly her mind flashed to Ethan. He was lost in the woods somewhere and she could only hope he was faring well. She wouldn't be leaving this island without him. But at least the others were saved.

The crowd grew more energetic and loud as the boats began towards them. Behind them there was a loud boom, it sounded like a cannon. Grace froze with most of the crowd, frowning as she tried to pinpoint where the noise had come from. She looked behind her quickly, wondering if it had come from the boats and echoed. It had sounded close. Suddenly she saw it, overhead a black shape zoomed in an arc towards the boats. It sent a wave of heat radiating down as it passed. The crowd froze in their cheers watching in horror as it struck the water with a resonating blast. Flames erupted across the waves between them and the boats. Grace turned to find Jerry in the, now frantic, crowd. He was nowhere to be seen.

For a moment she panicked, worried about his health as the crowd became rowdy with confusion. Bodies were tossed from side to side as they fought to catch a glimpse of the boats. In their desperation to be saved they had lost their group mentality, one thing had become very clear, every man for himself.

From the beach it appeared as though the boats themselves had burst into flames. She went silent with the others as they fought for a view, watching and waiting, hoping for the best. After a few baited moments a boat burst through the wall of fire, followed shortly by others. One of the boats appeared to have caught fire, they could see the scramble of the small figures jumping ship and climbing aboard another craft.

The beach filled with hushed whispers, concern for the boats that were their only hope. Some were wondering who was on board the fleet of vessels, others wondered how they had gotten to the island themselves if it was now so dangerous. What were their chances of getting off the island alive?

Their rescue had become a dangerous mission. The survivors watched with concern as the boats idled on this side of the tapering firewall. Soon the boats were plowing forward towards them again. Grace jumped and waived with excitement. Around her the beach erupted in cheers that almost drowned out the next explosion, almost.

She froze again, mid wave, as a funnel of water shot up capsizing one of the boats as it ripped it in half. She watched in horror as men flew through the air, debris surrounding their limp bodies. Grace and the others began backing away from the beach in shocked silence as the water settled. The path to the island was filled with explosives.

DETERMINATION

Jenny marched them towards the front door as she cleared the path with
her stick in hand. She slashed at any wire that crossed her way like she was
wielding an ax in the forest. When she finally reached the door, she began
kicking at it with enthusiasm. The resonating sounds of her footfalls on the
wood were loud considering the door barely shook on its hinges. Bruce
stared at her as though she were crazy.

"Doorknob?" He asked, pointing to the metal protrusion in the
door with a chuckle. He reached for it and Jenny slapped his hand back. He
looked up to her, startled at her quick reaction.

"It's probably electrified." She snipped with a raised brow. He
pulled his hand back quickly with understanding.

"Here." Bruce said as he guided her away from the door by her
shoulders with a show of his hands pointing to the forest. Backing up a few
paces himself, he took a running start at the door. Shoulder tucked in tight,
he cracked against the wood as it rattled against its frame with a groan.

Behind him there was a loud boom. He turned, believing he had
caused it. Through the clearing they could see the smoldering smoky mess
where something had detonated. The concern crossing Ethan and Jake's

faces was unnerving, there seemed to be nowhere safe on this damned island. He took another run for the door, this time with more determination.

The door splintered in protest as his shoulder pounded against the hard surface for a second time. He could tell he was hurt from the impact, but it seemed to have worked. He had knocked loose a large section of the rotting wood. It clung to the door still, sunken in and emitting a fine cloud of dust.

He began kicking at it with enthusiasm, watching as the wood finally gave way, turning into a foot-sized hole. Ethan took over when he tired, kicking at the edges of the hole until it had grown enough in size for them to enter.

Jenny watched from the front stoop trying to see through the hole as it became larger. She could see Colt's face now. She wondered why he was still in the cabin, it had taken them so long to break through the door and they hadn't been very quiet doing so. He had had plenty of time to escape.

Ethan stood at the door for a moment panting as he watched Colt inside. Colt stood with a tired smile splayed across his ragged face, the overwhelming scent of coffee wafted out to greet them. Ethan stood tall for a moment, straightening out his shoulders as he stared in at Colt before stooping down to enter the cabin. Bruce was quick to follow, keeping Jake behind him for his safety.

As Ethan righted himself on the other side of the door he stood mere feet away from the man who had been dragging him through this hell for the past five years. He could feel his heart beating heavily in his chest.

Colt didn't look intimidating. He was not a big brute of a man as Ethan had expected. His scrawny drawn out face had the look of a college professor who had gone off the deep end after grading one too many mediocre papers. Ethan stared for a moment longer, missing Colt's reaction as he raised his arm from his side.

"Ethan!" Bruce called peering from behind him.

It was too late, Colt had pulled the trigger.

***

Chung was terrified. He pulled a life jacket over his vest with no protest as he watched splinters of the boat ahead of them fluttering through the air like autumn leaves. The air-born men hit the water with smacking splashes, unable to prepare themselves in their unconscious state for the impact against the surface of the water.

There was a moment of panic on board as the crew searched the foaming waves for the bodies of their fallen comrades. Chung watched remorsefully as the crew began to bring them in.

The captain was reeling them in one at a time, hooking the limp bodies under their arms as the crew helped him heave them upwards onto the deck. Most of them had likely perished in the initial explosion, although the coroner would probably not rule out drowning.

Chung looked down in respect for the men that had fallen in their efforts. When he and King were involved the casualties always seemed to be high. Chung stepped forward to help pull the last ones aboard. This had just become one of the most dangerous missions he had ever embarked on. The stakes were ever growing with a full crew on the boats and the surviving passengers of the plane crash on the island, and his sister had still not appeared on the beach to appease his anxieties.

With all the water obstacles they had already encountered it was safe to assume the rest of the trip was likely to be a dangerous one. Chung had grown restless with fear. He paced the deck while he waited for the water to settle.

In Chung's mind an explosion on land was a low risk, the

possibility of unconsciousness on land was something survivable. As he looked out to the waves he realized that even a brief loss of consciousness on the water would result in immediate death by drowning. Add in his inability to swim in the first place and suddenly he was a prime target. The thought chilled him as he watched the island with concern, wondering how many of the passengers aboard the plane had suffered that same fate.

Water foamed as it crashed against the hull, the explosion had set them rocking in the water. They were close to capsizing as a wave exploded over the deck, knocking Chung from his feet as he grabbed onto the nearest rope in fear. Water cascaded across the deck, sending a chill up his spine as it washed over his stiff body. Around him the recovered bodies floated, bouncing against his legs as he held tight.

As the boat righted itself and the water fell back into the rocking waves he stood quickly, jumping away from the lifeless corpses of the other crew, nearly slipping off the side of the boat in his haste to get away.

Around them the other boats had cut their engines in an effort to save the crew that had gone overboard. King watched the silent shore through his binoculars. The survivors stood watching with gaping mouths as the fleet of rescue ships slowly went down one at a time.

King frowned, there had to be a safe way to get to shore without being blown out of the water. He watched as the last crew member was dragged from the foaming waves after a high wave nearly knocked them all back overboard again.

He took one of the poles from a crew member and hooked in a piece of the broken boat. As he pulled it out of the water he searched the waves for a likely spot to toss the debris, hoping to overcome any other water mines without damaging any more crew. He walked the deck searching the waves for the best place to aim. At the bow he decided to let loose the heavy piece of boat in his arms. He prayed that it had enough weight to affect any mines in the vicinity with its impact. He clung to the rail, bracing for impact and the resulting wave that he hoped for with his eyes closed.

With a splash the piece hit the water. It was followed closely by a funnel of water exploding before them, sending a wave of water flowing over the boats as it rocked the crew on board. The captain turned to King with a frown. Covered in water, he fumed.

"Why did you do that?" He waved his arms wildly with exasperation.

King shrugged, "I thought it would clear our path, wouldn't you rather find them before they explode on us?" He leaned back out over the boat with a hook in his hand to pull in another piece of debris. The captain closed his eyes, shaking his head with frustration.

"Do what the agent tells you." He yelled gruffly to the remaining crew as he turned his back to King so he could grab his radio.

Soon the rest of the crew were reaching for floating boat pieces, launching them into the air before the boat, spirals of water exploded one after another. Soon they had learned that the larger and heavier the piece was the better chance they had of triggering a mine. They began working in teams of two or three. Pulling the pieces from the water was the hardest part, the slippery masses of debris were hard to raise out of their watery bed and the threat of damage to their own vessel was a consideration they could not afford to overlook.

With heaving motions they tossed one piece after another over the bow, clearing a reasonably large area in the front so they could sneak forward and continue on the farther in areas.

Within a few minutes the other boats had begun to follow suit, using King's method to backtrack and fall into a line of sorts, the less area they had to cover the more likely it would be that they could clear it safely.

King watched with anxiety. If his method failed, he was on the first boat through the danger zone. They needed this to be successful.

Soon they would be safe to make their way through. The water was wild with rocking explosions, sending them tilting side to side as they fought to keep their footing while they worked. The path to the island was finally becoming clear as they inched forward one minute at a time.

CONFRONTATION

Ethan hit the hard floor loudly, a cloud of dust erupted around him as he twitched and withered under the influence of the Taser gun held firmly in Colt's hand. He had bitten his tongue as he had fallen, the trickle of blood escaping his mouth nearly choked him as he fought against the current contorting his body against his will.

"I don't think so buddy." Bruce growled as he crossed the room to Colt, slapping the device from his hand. Colt looked up with surprise, he hadn't expected Ethan's companion to be so bold.

Ethan continued to twitch for a moment as Jenny stooped down to help him remove the prongs from his shirt.

"Are you alright?" She asked slowly, watching him warily as she used her shirt to wipe the blood from his chin. His face was pale and he was stiff with pain. He managed a nod as she helped him get to his feet, leaning his body on hers for support.

Ethan scowled as he regained feeling in his limbs, the Taser had been worse than the electrified fence he had encountered at the amusement park, his skin felt hot and tingly. Slowly he righted himself, peeling away from Jenny as he stepped farther into the cabin towards Bruce and Colt.

The sinister smile that had been painted across Colt's face when he had pulled the Taser out had disintegrated into a stone faced snarl.

"Welcome Ethan," he snarled with twinkling eyes, "I see you have made some new friends."

Bruce shot him a look of shocked confusion, "You know him?" He whispered quietly to himself as he passed another look to Jake who was entering the cabin behind them.

Ethan ignored Bruce for a moment, keeping his eyes on Colt. Though he had never met him before, a sensation radiated off of Colt indicating that they had been foes for a long while. Ethan wondered how long Colt had been watching his life, and more importantly why? Had Colt been watching him since Grace's kidnapping, or had he picked up his trail somewhere later? Ethan's brain was spinning as the room settled into an awkward silence. The others were watching both he and Colt as they stared at one another.

Jenny stepped forward, passing Ethan as she closed in on Colt. He barely flinched as she slapped him straight across the face. "That's for my brother." She shouted as she wound up for another blow.

Colt snapped up her arm mid swing as though he were swatting away a fly. He broke his eye contact with Ethan, looking to the spectacle in front of him as though he had just realized she was in the room.

"I haven't even started yet." He smiled, backing behind his desk of monitors as he pushed her hand away lazily. "The game had only just begun."

Jenny tried to follow him around his desk, she was furious that he had dismissed her so easily and she felt secure knowing that there were three people to back her up and he was on his own. She had barely made it around the corner of the desk when Colt looked up to her with stony eyes, she was ready to continue walking until she saw the gun in his hand, held at his waist and pointed upwards at her body. She froze, taking a step back silently to fall in line with Ethan and Bruce.

Colt pressed a button on the intricate panel splayed across his desk lazily, staring at Jenny with amusement. Slowly he righted himself, walking back towards them with his gun held at waist level, pointed at the small group that had heroically broken into his cabin, effectively falling for another trap.

"Are you ready for the show?" He asked rhetorically as he glanced back at his monitors. With a slow movement he turned the central monitor to face them.

Ethan was silent as he looked at the screen, trying to figure out what he was looking at. It was a view of the water, from somewhere on the beach, looking outward into the rocky waves. A haze of smoky fire had covered the edge of the horizon. Ethan looked up at Colt with confusion, waiting to see what he was getting at.

Quietly Jenny gasped and Ethan turned his gaze back towards the monitor. He could now see tiny vessels far away on the screen, making their way towards the island through the smoke screen. His body stiffened as he thought of the boom they had heard outside of the cabin. He stared at the smoke on the monitor and instantly realized that their chance of rescue was in peril.

Across the room Colt chuckled as he watched Ethan piecing it all together. He glanced at the monitor briefly watching as the boats broke through the first of many obstacles. If things went as he planned, help would never reach the mainland. Colt was suddenly giddy with excitement as he watched the first mine explode, sending a plume of silent water upwards. He could almost hear their screams.

Jenny reached for Ethan's arm suddenly as she watched the water erupt on the screen. Tiny dots of debris fluttered back towards the waiting waves as she clung tightly to Ethan, tears welled up in her eyes.

"Ethan," she whispered frantically, "I can't watch." She said as she turned her face from the sight, tears silently streaming down her dirty face leaving trails in the filth.

Ethan stood tall beside her, knowing that Agents King and Chung would be aboard one of the boats he was watching on the screen. He only hoped they had enough sense to turn back while they still could.

Finally satisfied, Colt stepped forward. He approached Bruce first, holding a black zip-tie with a sneer, "You first big guy, hands out front."

Bruce was too shocked and absorbed in the chaos on-screen to care as he held his hands before him, wincing as Colt tightened the tie and it cut into his wrists. Colt gave the tie one last look before stepping sideways to Jake. As he zip-tied each of their hands he had a sense of closure, he was about to complete his masterpiece. He had expected Ethan to have more fight left in him, perhaps he had overestimated his abilities.

With the lot of them bound, Colt felt he was ready to embark on the last leg of his journey, he ventured to the back of the room where a large black case had been placed. He had been waiting for this moment for so long he could taste it. He took a deep breath in as he wiped a thin layer of dust off the top of the metal lid. He ran his hand across the smooth metal one last time before he clicked the latches open on the side. Exhaling slowly, he lifted the lid.

Colt stared in at the flame thrower he had acquired some years prior. He had won it in a very sketchy deal that had nearly cost him his life. He had waited for the perfect moment to unleash it on the masses, today would be perfect. He could almost see himself, a phoenix rising from the ashes as he claimed his place in the world. He would be better than Hart could have imagined, he would be unrivaled, he would be free.

***

Ethan searched the cabin for something to loosen his tie. Colt had retreated to the back of the small room, hidden behind his monitors and gadgets. Ethan watched as he continued to be distracted by something at the back of the room, Colt was pulling pieces from a case in the back, assembling something. Ethan seized the opportunity to look around the remainder of the cabin knowing that he needed to find a way to get to the beach and warn the others, he needed to stop Colt from completing his master plans. But first he needed to get free.

The small group had been left standing against the wall inside the cabin by the door, their legs were free but they knew Colt still had his gun and would be quicker than them with his arms unbound, escaping into the woods was not an option they were willing to take. Even if they did manage to all outrun Colt, there was the worry of traps and other dangers out in the woods that could just as easily kill them.

Ethan feared that moving might catch Colt's attention and it was a risk he wasn't willing to take, slowly he moved his foot, fighting to keep his balance so Colt wouldn't notice him moving. He could see the remnants of the Taser scattered across the entranceway and hoped that he could use some of the metal from the prongs to cut through the tie Colt had placed on his wrists.

Finally his foot caught hold of a wire, slowly he began to pull it back towards him, watching Colt's movement out of the corner of his eye to be sure he wasn't aware. The rotting floor provided cover for what should have been a scraping motion as Ethan hooked the wire again after catching a snag in the soft wood. Slowly but surely he was managing to get the device across the floor towards him. He wasn't sure what he would be able to do once he had it, one look from Colt and it would all be over.

When he had the Taser at his feet he glanced back to Colt, he was standing now, pulling something heavily out of a crate and onto his back. It looked like some sort of canister from the back, painted a camouflage green, it looked military.

"A flamethrower?" Bruce whispered from beside him in awe. Colt looked back at the sound to be sure his hostages held still.

Bruce went stiff as his eyes made contact with Colt's cold steel stare. He looked down quickly to avoid a confrontation with the mad man holding a flamethrower.

Slowly Colt walked back through the room, pausing for a moment at the line of monitors still facing the back of the room. One at a time, he turned them to face his visitors. Then with a small smile he walked to the door, tucking his pistol into his waistband as he reached for the door handle.

"Enjoy the show." He chided as he opened the broken door and stepped into the outside world, leaving them alone in the dilapidated cabin.

Ethan listened as the crunch of his footsteps receded into the woods, until he thought Colt was far enough away to bend over to get the Taser. As Ethan fumbled with the prongs on the Taser, the others were watching the screens. Ethan refused to glance up, he needed to get out of the ties and back to the beach before Colt had a chance to toast the survivors.

Ethan grasped the prong in one hand, twisting it to hook onto the tie at his wrist. After several tries, his arm was dripping with blood and the tie was still almost fully intact. He fought against the pain and the slipping grip he had on the small piece of hooked metal as he struggled to finish.

Beside him Bruce had stooped to pick up the other prong. Watching Ethan, he began to cut through his own tie with ease.

Soon the two were free, Ethan raced to the door with only a fleeting glance back as he called to Jenny.

"I'll meet you at the beach." He yelled as he and Bruce raced from the cabin.

"Go!" Jenny and Jake called after them, looking at the screens with worry. Whatever Colt was planning, Grace and the others were just sitting ducks.

CHALLENGE

Ethan and Bruce raced through the woods without direction. They followed what appeared to be a path, hoping desperately that this was the route that Colt had chosen to get to the beach.

Ethan hoped that they were right in assuming that with his heavy gear, Colt would have chosen the easiest path through. He was rewarded a moment later when he spotted the heavy backpack up ahead, attached to it was Colt.

Ethan jumped through the forest with reverence as he and Bruce closed in on their target. Ahead, Colt had noticed the rustling in the bushes behind him. He turned sharply, holding the wand of the device with both hands.

Colt fumbled in his pocket for a moment trying to ignite the torch hastily as the two closed in on him. Before he had a chance to get the torch lit Ethan was on him, throwing himself recklessly through the brush to tackle Colt to the ground.

They hit the ground with a thud, Colt fought against the restraint of the canister on his back as he tried to get the upper hand on Ethan. He swung out heavily with the wand of the flamethrower, striking his opponent on the side of the face with a slap. Ethan recoiled at the impact as he struggled to remain on top of Colt while waiting for Bruce to catch up.

As they rocked back and forth on the ground, Colt struggled against the weight of his back piece. He knew he wouldn't be able to throw Ethan off with the added pressure of the device pulling him back. He tried to free a hand to release the buckle across his chest, but Ethan was holding his hands fast at his sides, using his knees to press them against the ground as he sat atop Colt.

Colt was all but immobile, he bucked upwards hoping to lose Ethan. Soon Bruce arrived and restrained his legs, feeling into Colt's pockets smartly for the pistol he had brandished at the cabin. Quickly he held the gun in his own hand, nodding to Ethan with relief.

"Take off the pack." Bruce told Ethan as he swooped towards Colt's head, aiming the gun towards him to keep him from giving a fight.

Ethan fumbled with the buckles crossing Colt's body, many of them had become tangled while they had been fighting. Ethan ripped at the last of the ties triumphantly, releasing Colt from the backpack as he stared up at him with cold eyes.

"Tie his hands with some of the bindings." Bruce suggested as Ethan tore off the last of the pack's fasteners.

"Yeah I got it." Ethan replied, loosening one of his knees to gain access to Colt's hand. He grabbed quickly, fearing that Colt was ready to strike back, but with Bruce holding a gun over them he suspected Colt was playing possum until he could find a way to escape. Ethan wasn't about to let him have that chance. He ripped off the shoulder straps that were still attached to the canister under Colt's stiff body, using them to bind his hands together. When he was sure that they were secure he moved to Colt's legs, sitting atop his knees to prevent Colt from kicking up at him. He knew it would only take one moment for Colt to regain control, Ethan worked quickly.

When he was sure he had Colt tied up and incapacitated he hopped up to join Bruce.

"We should take him to the beach." Ethan suggested as he caught his breath. Bruce was quick to disagree.

"Why shouldn't we just shoot him right here? The guy is crazy, look at all the stuff he did, he was ready to blowtorch an entire beach filled with people. Why should he live?" Bruce was pacing now, he shook with rage as he thought of all of the people that had gone down in that plane crash, what had happened to his best man Jake. He was supposed to be marrying the girl of his dreams, instead he was here on this island with a rampant killer. He breathed heavily trying to shake the feeling, he wanted to shoot that man, without mercy while his hands were tied. Part of him knew that wasn't the answer, he looked to Ethan for advice hoping he could talk some sense into him. He knew if Ethan agreed with him he would pull the trigger, the thought startled him.

"We should take him to the beach." Ethan said again, firmer this time as Bruce continued to pace before him. He could see his companion shaking as he contemplated murder, Ethan hoped he was a better man than that. He walked forward, keeping an eye on Colt as he approached Bruce. He held his hand firmly out, for Bruce to hand over the weapon, praying he had made the right choice.

Bruce paused in his loop around the clearing, looking at Ethan's outstretched hand in a daze. Slowly he moved towards him, gun held low at his side. With a deep breath, he held it out towards Ethan's outstretched hand. He paused for a moment, keeping the pistol in his grasp as he looked Ethan in the eyes.

"How do you know him?" Bruce spoke firmly, demanding answers before he would relinquish his weapon to Ethan.

Ethan was unsure how to answer, it was a long story to say the least. How could he convey in one sentence the torment that Colt had put him through over the last several years, the loss and the struggle that he had endured as he had fought to keep his life from spiraling into hell? Bruce was staring at him now, waiting for an explanation, and a reason why he should give Ethan the gun.

Ethan dropped his shoulder as he finally answered, "We were on our way to a safe house," he explained, "because of him." He pointed to Colt, hoping that Bruce would accept his brief story without asking for further detail.

Bruce paused for a moment, looking back at Colt with surprise. He had been expecting something different, Ethan could tell he was relieved.

"Well, I can see why." He whispered as he placed the pistol into Ethan's hand. "Let's get him to the beach." He finally agreed.

Ethan nodded appreciatively as he checked the gun over, unsure how to secure the safety. Finally he tucked it into his back pocket and joined Bruce in heaving Colt's withering body upwards so they could carry him towards the beach.

Ethan let Bruce take the lead, he had reached for Colt's feet leaving Ethan to take up the upper half of his body. He could tell Colt was trying to make this uncomfortable for him, staring up at him he whispered quietly. Ethan strained to hear, while pretending he hadn't noticed.

"...your father won't make it.....the agents are lost..." Each word out of Colt's mouth was more infuriating than the last "...Grace is gone..."

Ethan bit his tongue as he held his face stiffly, looking upwards at the path ahead to avoid losing his grasp on Colt. He couldn't let him get under his skin, one slip up and Colt would be back on the top. With an island full of traps, he was still a force to be reckoned with.

***

Jenny had finally gotten her hands free. She turned to help Jake, knowing that his shoulder injury would make it more difficult for him to maneuver the spike on his own. His face was pale and drenched in a fine mist of sweat as the pressure on his wound became unbearable.

"How's your shoulder?" Jenny asked quietly as she tried to free his hands. She could tell he was biting his lip in silent protest to the pain.

"Just be quick." He begged, eyes rolling back in his head as Jenny bumped his arm sending a shooting pain into his shoulder.

When she had freed his arms she turned to look at the contents of the cabin. Ethan and Bruce had hopefully reached Colt by now, the monitors on the beach hadn't shown his fiery arrival yet so there was still time. She stared at the screens with wonder, thinking that if she had more knowledge of the set-up she might be able to disable some of the traps from within the cabin. She turned to Jake, wondering if he could handle more time in the cabin.

"I think I'm going to stay for a while and see if I can get some of this shut down." She announced, walking to take a seat in Colt's chair. She turned the monitors back towards her so she could watch while she figured it out. If Jake wanted to leave, she would be okay. Silently she hoped he would stay.

Jake chuckled, pushing a crate with his foot towards Jenny, he plopped himself down beside her, "Let's do this." He nodded with strained enthusiasm, pulling a stack of papers towards himself with his good arm. Maybe Colt had left some notes to help them figure out what all of the dials controlled.

"Thanks." Jenny smiled, picking up another stack of pages.

As she looked through them she became more concerned. The papers not only contained a passenger manifesto from their flight, but communications with the control center, background checks on some of the passengers on board and others who had been conveniently moved to other flights, including a nurse and a Sargent. Colt had put a lot of time and effort into making sure that they landed on this island in particular, he had been on board the plane himself as the co-captain.

"Look at this." Jenny said, holding the last page up to Jake so he could see it. It was a copy of the passenger manifesto, with red lines through names of the deceased, detailed in small red letters beside their names was how they had died. Beside several uncrossed names were injuries he had inflicted, at the bottom was a detailed summary of the turmoil the rescue boats were about to encounter.

"Oh my..." Jake went paler than he had already been. He looked at the dials before them frantically trying to decide how to cut the function of the switches. "How can we stop it?" He looked to Jenny for an answer, tears were streaming down her face silently.

"Jenny?" He asked her softly, wondering why it was now that she was breaking.

Slowly she looked back to him with a fire in her eyes that sent a chill up his spine. With a frantic energy she ripped the pages from before him, flipping through them with rapid speed. Soon she had found what she was looking for.

Quickly she unfolded a chart before her, it had the image of the control panel on it and beside some of the switches were little red notes detailing what they controlled. With a flick on the board, she had changed the monitors to reflect the dock of the beach. From there she could see the boats in the distance and the survivors waving frantically as they waited for help to arrive.

"I think this will stop the explosion under the dock." She said pointing to a dial on the chart as she held it for Jake to see. Suddenly she was all business. He nodded in agreement, watching as she flicked the corresponding dial from on to off. He watched the screen with rapt attention, waiting for the blast to consume them. It appeared that it had been a timed event, he prayed that they had deterred it from happening.

After a moment he was satisfied that they had prevented the dock disaster. He exhaled heavily, smiling at Jenny as she stared at the chart with concentration. When she didn't glance back at him he took it as a sign that she was busy. He turned back to the monitor to watch the progress of the boats, moving slowly but surely through the wild waves, smartly detonating one mine after another while staying safe on board. Jake watched them with fascination, the rescue boats seemed to have a plan to get them to shore.

As Jake and Jenny disassembled Colt's getaway cabin, they came to realize that they were still vulnerable to any of his remote traps. The detailed lists told them that there were covered holes, mines and arrows throughout the woods.

"We should head out, Bruce might need some help with that guy." Jake announced a few minutes after they had finished shutting down the computers. With the blank monitors staring back at them it suddenly felt very unsafe in the cabin. A silent chill had set in and Jenny looked spooked.

"Yeah, let's get outta here." She agreed, looking warily at the four corners of the small space. She raced out of the door, only pausing once she had reached the fresh air outside to wait for Jake.

He was walking slowly, not out of fatigue but out of concern for his shoulder injury. Every movement sent a piercing spike of pain through him. He would be relieved when he was able to get the arrow out of his shoulder. He hoped that the rescue boats had come equipped to deal with this kind of injury, he worried that the longer it was in the more painful it would be to get it back out.

Jenny stared at the woods before them, wondering which way the others had traveled. Colt had likely taken the safest path, so that would be their best bet. But which way had he gone?

"Jake, do you know which way they went?" She asked, praying that he had been able to see out of the cabin door when Ethan and Bruce had gone running off after Colt. Ethan would have known the best way to go.

Jake thought for a moment, looking back to the cabin as though he were calculating it out in his mind. "Somewhere over that way," he said pointing to half of the area before them, "I'll bet they took the path, Colt would have needed it with that gear he had on." He finally nodded.

Jenny smiled, "Genius." She smirked, starting forward. Jake was right, with all that gear Colt would have stayed on a path rather than dragging his pack through the brush.

She and Jake quickly fell into pace, traveling on the path back to the beach warily, watching the way for a sign that Bruce and Ethan had caught up to Colt. The silence in the woods was refreshing.

EAGER

Grace watched the dark foaming mass buck and sway in raging waves as the massive explosions sent the water swirling around towards them. She stared at the foamy mess as it washed over the creaking dock, threatening to swipe it down with one wave. Some of the others had traveled out onto the rattling dock to get a better view of the boats. Grace had stayed on shore with Jerry, the wood looked decayed. One strong breeze could probably turn it to dust. But the few who were brave enough were standing at the edge waving frantically at the boats as they approached, foamy waves crashing at their feet.

The explosions got closer as the boats closed in on the beach, and with the smaller space between shore and the mines, the waves were increasing in size. It started slowly, first the waves were crashing at the dock. Soon they were arching over the planks and washing away pieces of the crackling wood, one beam at a time. The few that had used the space to gain perspective on the boats were now panicking as they tried to get back to shore without being swept into the raging water.

With one last explosion from offshore, the dock began to buckle into the water, taking with it the survivors that had ventured out to watch from the edge. Grace looked on as the decaying wood collapsed around them. They turned to the beach in horror, scrambling to get ashore before the dock disappeared under the angry foaming water. It lapped against their legs as they struggled over the warping wood and splinters to the shore.

Suddenly the cheers of joy that had overtaken the beach upon the arrival of the fleet had turned dark. Shrieks of horror and fear surrounded Grace and Jerry as they clung together on the beach. Above them the bright sun mocked their pain.

Grace watched, as before her eyes a foaming wave lapped over those trying to return to the beach, the dock and the two men disappeared with the slap of a single crash of water. Grace rushed forward pulling Jerry with her for fear of losing him again in the chaos.

"Find them!" She called to the gasping crowd as they stood in shock, gaping at the water edge. Her voice spurred them on, giving them a purpose as they raced to the shore, searching for a sign of their lost companions in the rising tide. Someone else had taken over, barking orders at the small gathering by the dock. Soon they were making a chain to gather the two stranded men clinging to the docks pillars in the angry water. Before the chain could enter the water another wave struck the beams. The crowd backed away from the shore with uncertainty.

The rocking explosions continued by the boats, the water was dark with refuse and foam, not a sign of the missing men in the murky water. Grace thought of diving in to search, knowing that she wouldn't be able to find them in the angry water held her back. She continued to stare with sorrow. They were gone, if they had only held out a few more minutes they could have been saved.

Grace backed slowly from the shore, over the wet rocks towards the waiting crowd. Jerry walked with her to the back of the crowd, watching the water and the boats with strong resolve. He barely noticed when Grace placed her hand on his elbow to speak to him.

"They're gone." She whispered.

Suddenly her mind was worrying again about Ethan and Jenny in the wilderness. She hoped they were in the wilderness and not...She shook the thought from her head, joining Jerry in his vigilant watch of the boats. He had been silent the whole time, watching the boats making their way towards the shore as though he were keeping tabs on how many lives were lost. They had both hoped that King and Chung were on board, and with Jerry's watchful eye he would know which boat they were on before they reached the shore. He held Grace's hand firmly as they closed in slowly moving against the raging water.

The boats had formed a conga line of sorts, after the first water mine had gone off. One boat was now in the lead, tossing debris into the waves to clear a path for the others to follow. Grace wondered if this was a common occurrence, they seemed to be handling the disturbance with ease. Though it slowed them, detonating each mine before moving forward, they were still making good progress.

She could see that they were running out of usable debris to set off the mines and they were so close to shore. Her heart ached as she wondered what they would do. It took her a minute to figure it out. They had stopped, and at a standstill they were watching the water unmoving. From her vantage it appeared that they had frozen, save for the rocking of the water beneath them. Then she saw from the boat behind them they were transferring a heavy parcel. They had run out of debris and were using the sandbags from the other boats to continue forward. She could see now the tiny brigade passing sandbags from one boat to another and all the way to the front of the first vessel. They were going to make it after all. Grace smiled to Jerry.

"They should be here soon." She whispered with a huge smile. Jerry squeezed her hand and smiled back.

She looked back to the line of boats with excitement, eager to get aboard and head back to the mainland. As she stared at the line she watched the rear two boats slowly back up and turn around.

"No." She whispered as they disappeared slowly over the horizon. What was going on? Her mouth hung open as she feared they were about to give up. The boats left at the back of the line were stalling, not keeping pace with the others.

What had once been eight boats had slowly diminished to six. If they continued to lose vessels they wouldn't be able to fit all the waiting passengers on the beach. As it was they would need to do more than one trip. No one would want to be on the second run, no one wanted to be on this island any longer than they needed to be.

Grace stared at the boats past Jerry's shoulder, scouring the crew in the front vessel, hopeful to see the two faces she knew would come to their rescue. She scanned each boat in turn, trying to take in the build and stature of each passenger to compensate for the distance and boat movement stealing her chance to see their faces properly.

She was still praying that Jenny was okay and would be back before Chung reached the shore. If she was not there when they came ashore Grace couldn't bear to tell him the bad news. She still refused to believe herself that Jenny might be lost to her. Ethan was out there somewhere, but what had he found?

She covered her eyes from the glaring sun as the boats came closer. She could see a man on the first boat watching through binoculars. He hadn't moved from his spot despite the rocking of the boats. He stood stiffly, holding a railing for support as he clutched the binoculars to his eyes with determination. Grace couldn't make out his features from the distance, but she had a strong feeling it was Chung, looking for his sister. Guilt welled up inside her as she wondered what he was feeling. She held Jerry's hand tighter, knowing she wasn't ready to face him just yet.

***

Bruce and Ethan were struggling to make it to the beach from the cabin. The weight of Colt's body was a burden that they shared, one taking his feet the other his arms. Soon after they had reached the main trail the struggle had become more profound as he tried frantically to escape his bindings. Ethan lost his grip on Colt's shoulders as he wiggled frantically before him. Colt slipped from his hands with a deafening crack. Ethan looked up to Bruce as he spun around in shock.

"Sorry, he just slipped." Ethan apologized as he reached down to retrieve Colt. He had stopped squirming and lay motionless on the forest floor. Ethan paused for a moment, checking his breathing before attempting to lift him back up.

"He's bleeding." Bruce noted, setting Colt's legs to the ground to check the side of Colt's head where he had seen a glistening red dripping.

"Oh, damn." Ethan watched as Bruce turned Colt's head to the side, revealing a sizable wound, dripping with blood.

"Does that mean he's out cold?" Bruce asked, flicking Colt on the nose to see him react. Colt remained still, "I guess so." He looked up to Ethan for confirmation.

"I guess we keep going?" Ethan reached again for Colt's shoulders, relieved that he wouldn't have to fight against his struggling body as he walked through the woods. He didn't think he had the energy to struggle any more, he was tiring quickly. Only the thought of Grace and the boats kept him going as he staggered through the woods following Bruce's lead.

Colt suddenly snapped awake, jolting his body as he regained consciousness for a moment. The shock of the unexpected movement nearly caused Ethan to drop him again. He held tight as Colt stared at him with wild eyes for a moment before slowly rolling his eyes back in his head and going limp again.

Bruce paused, sensing a shift in Colt's weight, "Everything alright?" He called back to Ethan.

"Yeah, he woke up for a second." Ethan called back, securing his grip on Colt's shoulders in case he awoke again. Bruce nodded gruffly to the forest before him.

"'kay." He said starting forward again.

Suddenly their journey through the dense forest became more troublesome as Colt began slipping in and out of consciousness. Ethan had the benefit of seeing his eyes moving slowly beneath the lids before he awoke. Bruce was having more trouble with the process, the sudden movements causing him to drop Colt several times when he struggled too harshly in his restlessness.

The winding wire they had followed in to get to the cabin had provided them with an obstacle riddled path, yet it had been passable. The main path before them was devious, misleading and more dangerous than Ethan would have expected. It gave the illusion of a pathway, but it had been unused for such a long time that it had become overgrown in areas, Bruce and Ethan were having trouble deciphering the paths windy nature. Areas that looked like they were clear soon became dead ends, sending them backtracking through the brush to find the original path and start over. Other areas were leaden with swampy marshes, making it all the more difficult to carry Colt's weight as they trudged through ankle deep muck.

As heavy as Colt was in his silence, it became more trouble to untangle his prone form from the bushes in their quest to return to the others.

Bruce in the lead, kept a vigilant watch for other obstacles that might hinder their progress. He had learned by now that the island was riddled with more man-made obstructions than they had already discovered. Though it would be amusing to see the bound scoundrel succumb to one of his own traps, Bruce wasn't willing to make that sacrifice with his own life, he had a bride to get to.

Ethan was listening for Jenny and Jake catching up to them, he was sure they were taking too much time. He wondered if they had managed to get out of their ties yet. With Jake's injured shoulder it may have taken them an extra minute, but they should have been catching up to him and Bruce by now, the two were traveling tediously slow through the brush. Jake and Jenny had nothing to slow them down. He glanced back nervously, wondering if they had taken a different path.

For all he knew they could be at the beach already, waiting for them as they told Grace of their heroic adventures through the island's interior.

Ethan let his mind wander to the boats he had seen coming in on the monitors at the cabin. Help had arrived and he wanted to get there before they left again. He was positive that King and Chung were aboard, the two would have jumped the second they realized the plane had gone down. Ethan doubted now that King had ever sent in the request for a safe house, surely the plane they had taken was not King's choosing. He glanced down at Colt, wondering how long this island scheme had been in the works.

Colt regained consciousness again and as he began to squirm making their task all the more tedious, Ethan lost his grip with a withering falter. Ethan had taken him under the arms following behind Bruce who had grasped both feet under one arm so he could lead the way. As Colt swung at the ground Bruce fell back from the sudden change in the weight.

"Hey." He called with surprise as Colt began squirming with reverence, fighting to get out of his bindings.

"Sorry." Ethan called ahead, trying to get Colt back into his grips. Colt looked at him with scowling rage, if it were not for the scrap of cloth that they had found to cover his mouth, Ethan was sure he would be spewing all kinds of horrid venom at them. The fabric had come from Ethan's shirt after the first drop of Colt, Ethan had tired of hearing him muttering under his breath and in his unconscious state he had half hoped Colt would suffocate and save him the trouble of a lengthy trial.

Now Colt looked as though he were ready to do his villainous speech. Ethan looked forward with a smirk, watching as Bruce righted himself, grasping Colt's legs. Silently the two continued on.

After a few more rough falls, Colt stopped wiggling about. He stared up at Ethan with dark cruel eyes. Ethan tried to avoid his stare. His haunting eyes burned into Ethan as they fumbled through the woods, if looks could kill Colt would have had his way already. He still tried to talk to Ethan as he was dragged through the woods, his seething rant coming out as a garble of moans through the rag in his mouth.

Ethan was dripping with sweat, worried that the winding path might be taking them in circles. Finally he called forward, "Do you see the beach yet?"

Bruce looked up from the path to see what was ahead of them. Stopping, he turned back to Ethan.

"I can see the trees thinning out, listen." He went quiet, listening ahead for sounds. The rush of water greeted them in the distance. Already they could hear the calls and shouts of the others mingling with the roar of the incoming waves. It was the best sound Ethan had heard all day. He struggled through his breathing to pinpoint the voice that he wanted to hear, Grace. He would have to get closer.

Ethan shifted his hold on Colt. His arms ached from the weight. His back was slouched over and burning in protest.

"Let's get going." He called as Bruce started forward again. After a minute of heavy breathing, Bruce let go, dropping his arm to his side he looked apologetically to Ethan.

"I'm going to need a minute, my arms are asleep." He shook them around trying to get feeling back. Ethan set Colt down with agreement.

"Yeah, mine are pretty sore too." He stretched up, relieving his back of the slouched strain.

"Do you think the others are at the beach already?" Bruce scanned behind them in the woods, searching for a rustling that would indicate whether Jake and Jenny were still in the woods with them.

"I bet they are." Ethan replied, rubbing his sore arms with resolve, "They didn't have to carry *him*." He kicked a foot at Colt squirming against his bonds on the ground between them.

"Very true." Bruce agreed.

On the ground, Colt wiggled, squirming to get to his feet beneath him. He fought against the gag on his mouth working his jaw like he needed to speak. Bruce and Ethan shared a look, knowing they couldn't take too much of a break without Colt getting the upper hand on them. They couldn't risk him getting free at this point, ahead was a beach full of stranded travelers, vulnerable and oblivious of the danger he posed. Behind them were Jenny and Jake, ill prepared to face Colt on their own. Especially Jenny, Colt would surely target her.

Rather than taking a longer break to relieve their aches and pains they switched ends. Ethan took Colt's feet and the lead, continuing towards the sound of water ahead.

UNEASE

The crew had cleared the path before the boats as best as they could. Chung had stood watching the beach as they made slow progress towards the shore. Two of the waiting passengers had been swept away when the rough waters had demolished the ratty dock beneath them. The crowd had retreated farther onto the dry sand.

He scanned their faces as they closed in, holding the binoculars to his face as he held himself steady against the railing. The fear radiated off of their waiting forms, even from this distance. He could tell they worried that the boats wouldn't make it to them, that they would be trapped forever. He continued to scan the far off crowd, one face at a time. After he had found Grace he was sure this was the place, these were the survivors from the plane.

"King!" He shouted across the deck, waiting impatiently for his companion to make his way across the tilting floor. "It's them," he relayed when his partner was close enough. "Grace is out there." He pointed to the island, turning back to his post with his binoculars in hand, watching the beach for the others. He still hadn't seen Jenny amongst the waiting crowd, his heart beat faster each time he saw someone pass his line of vision with similar features. Soon Jerry had appeared in the back beside Grace, holding her arm tightly. He scoured the area near the two familiar faces hoping to see Ethan or Jenny, some of the young men wandering the beach could have been Ethan, but none of them appeared to know Grace. He could tell by the way they were interacting with the crowd, something wasn't right.

He wasn't sure that Ethan was there either.

He called King over again with a wave, as the boat slowly plodded forward.

"I can't find Ethan or Jenny." He spoke slowly as King reached for the binoculars with shaking hands. He passed them over without a struggle. King took a stance holding onto the rail for support while he scanned the island himself. He frowned after several passes of the beach.

"That can't be all of them." He sounded sure, even as his voice wavered. Chung hadn't the heart to dispute him. He wanted to believe that there were more survivors too.

Soon they were closing in on the beach, without a dock to anchor to, the crew was left floundering in the rough waters to anchor the boats on the crooked posts that had once held the dock, slipping on the wet stones as they worked. They were all soaked from the rough ride in anyway, so most of the team began hopping overboard into the rough waters, wading to shore with totes tucked over their shoulders. With medical supplies and rations in tow, they splashed to the beach with effort and purpose, watching the water around themselves warily as they went.

When the crew reached shore, they scattered amongst the survivors dripping across the beach while they aided them with rations of food and medical treatments. Most were only sunburned and dehydrated. It was quick work to get them aboard the first boat. Soon it was filled with eager passengers.

The boat slowly turned, following as close to the original path as it could muster, gradually making its way towards the horizon to take them to the mainland, where real food and paramedics awaited them with the unavoidable media frenzy.

As the first boat disappeared over the horizon, it was replaced with a helicopter, bright orange the whirring of its engine was unmistakable. The beach erupted in cheers, as those afraid of the safety on board the boats were presented with an alternate way to get ashore.

The chopper swooped low to the island, hovering as it selected a landing site suitable for it and the large propellers atop it. The boat crews began herding survivors out of the way to make room, hopeful of getting this ordeal over in one trip.

The chopper filled the beach with a resounding whop of its engine as the crew on board began to evacuate, bringing with them stretchers and first aid packs. They had come to take the more severely injured. One of the boat technicians led them towards Jarred, still sitting on the beach. He was pale with exhaustion as his wounds festered in the heat. They were careful as they strapped him to their gurney and led him back to the chopper. Within minutes the orange helicopter had disappeared over the horizon, leaving behind some of its crew and an island full of hopeful passenger wanting to avoid the dangers of exploding aboard one of the boats.

The crew continued working in a flurry, Grace watched as the beach came alive before her. In a daze, she stared at the quick moving paramedics and listened to their shouts as they assessed the critical cases of dehydration and checked over crash induced wounds.

As the crew worked to carry the injured back to the boats on their floating stretchers, the sun beat down on them. The dark black of their jackets clinging, damp and hot, to their bodies as the relief of their rescue broke the survivors to tears.

It was emotional on the beach as they tried to round up the rest of the wreckage and secure more boats for the passengers from the dock on the mainland. The beach had become a chaotic way-station, everyone seemed in a hurry to get off of the island.

Chung and King raced for Grace, worried that she carried horrible news. She greeted them both with hugs. A medic was looking Jerry over beside her. He seemed worse for the wear, his bright red skin looked sore as it blistered and peeled from sun exposure.

Grace watched as the medic applied a cream to Jerry's sore skin, unable to focus on King and Chung in front of her. Her mind was reeling with the news that she needed to share with them, and whether she could stall for a moment longer. She prayed for a miracle.

Grace was pleased to see the two of them. She collapsed into them with relief. But she knew that Chung's darting eyes were looking for someone else. She pulled away, watching Chung's features as a fresh wave of guilt washed over her.

"She was in the back of the plane," Grace spoke quietly placing a hand on his arm for comfort in her awkward embrace, "Ethan and some others went to look for them." She glanced to the trees with sadness, "They haven't come back yet." Her features dropped as the words escaped her mouth, the promise of their survival seemed lost as it passed her lips.

Chung's face was drawn, he looked to the tree line hopefully distraught, "He's not back yet?" He commented quietly as he turned to catch Grace's face as it fell again.

"No," She watched him looking towards the trees, "but we heard noises in the woods..." she trailed off as she shuffled her foot in the sand trying to keep her hopes up, "and there are video cameras everywhere..." she looked to King this time, she could tell from his face that he had suspected Colt. "Jerry and I think it's Colt." She confirmed as King and

Chung scowled towards the trees.

"That would make the most sense, cameras and everything." He turned back to the waiting boats regarding the floating debris with remorse. "We should have anticipated this." He pulled out his phone, distracted, "No reception, of course." He frowned, tucking it away again. "The captain has a radio, I'll be back." He called over his shoulder as he raced across the beach to the captain. They would have to call in more backup for analyzing if Colt was in fact involved. He wanted to be sure there was a team ready.

As King rushed away there was a rustle in the trees, Grace and Chung stared. Quietly he pulled her behind his body, shielding her from an impending attack. She peeked over his shoulder as a strange mass emerged from the woods, Ethan was carrying a body. Her heart stopped, she could hear Chung pull in a deep breath as he marched forward, Grace followed.

Ethan looked up with a large smile splayed across his face, "About time, Chung." He nodded to the agent as the body behind him slowly emerged from the woods. It was not Jenny, Chung and Grace gasped as they realized it was a man. Grace didn't recognize him from the group that had joined Ethan in his expedition. She frowned.

"Who is that?" She stared over his shoulder as he and Bruce dropped the body heavily to the sand. She stepped forward quickly, trying to reach him in time to stop him from landing so heavily.

"Don't." Ethan cautioned, putting a hand between her and the man. "This is Colt." He announced to Chung, waving his other hand to show the body behind him.

Colt was bound and gagged, he was bleeding from the side of his head and the heavy breathing through his nostrils hardly concealed the growling coming from his mouth as he tried to speak.

Bruce stepped forward from behind Colt, "He was about to blowtorch the entire beach." He said, glancing warily back at Colt. "We stopped him just in time."

DESPAIR

Grace couldn't hide her disappointment, tears streamed down her face silently as she thought of the ordeal Ethan had just gone through. He had confronted Colt. He and Bruce looked battered and worn, more damaged than those who had stayed on the beach and there were only two of them now. She looked over Ethan's shoulder into the woods wondering where the rest of his team had gone to, knowing that Colt had probably killed them all. To make it worse, Jenny was still gone. They must not have found the tail end of the plane, or there were no survivors left to find.

Ethan pulled Grace in close, stroking her hair as she wept, "We found Colt, Grace." Ethan whispered serenely. He seemed calmer than he should given the gravity of the situation, perhaps he was suffering from exhaustion, or shock. Grace stared up at him with confusion.

Chung marched past, pointing aggressively at the tied man, "This is him?" He asked with resolve. Ethan nodded.

Chung stooped down picking the man up with one arm under his chin, the collar on his shirt ripped in protest, "This is for my sister." He whispered as he held him up. Colt's eyes went wide. He squirmed in protest as Chung brought his other fist up to meet Colt in the chin. He rose an inch off of the ground before collapsing back down in a heap. Chung grabbed him by the feet, dragging him heavily through the sand towards King on the lower beach, leaving a trench in his wake. Colt squirmed in protest as his face plowed through the damp sand.

King looked up when Chung approached with the body, staring in horror at the disrespect his partner was showing for these suffering survivors.

"Chung..." He said with reprimand, gesturing towards the man he was dragging with raised eyebrows, "A little respect?" He muttered.

Chung tossed the feet down in the sand, "This is Colt." He spoke gruffly, like he was holding back an intense desire to kill the man with his bare hands right there on the beach.

King's face turned to stone as he watched Chung kick a foot at the quivering mass at his feet. He appeared to be holding himself together with rage, there had still been no sign of Jenny amongst the survivors. Even after Ethan had appeared on the beach, he suspected the worst.

King leaned down to have a look. He had expected more of this Colt character that had been eluding them for so long. Sure he had a look about him that said he was intelligent, clever even. But he didn't look like the sort that was capable of making elaborate plans like this on his own. He looked like a lackey.

"Where did you find him?" He finally asked, righting himself and brushing the sand from his knees.

Chung thrust a finger to the trees, "Ethan brought him out." He was curt and King supposed this was his way of dealing with the loss of his sister. King turned his head as he beamed, trying to keep his joy to himself.

"Ethan, is he okay?" King asked, starting to walk up to the tree line where he stood with Grace and some others. He didn't wait for a response and Chung wasn't about to give him one.

Instead Chung stood still, guarding the man that had cost his sister her life. Colt would pay for what he had done, and Chung would be there every step of the way to make sure he was paying in full.

"Hey Kid!" King called as he reached Ethan. Grace was busy in conversation with another man. Ethan seemed relieved for some company as he turned his back to them, pulling King on for a pat on the back.

"So glad to see you." Ethan said. His face was bloody and his body battered, but the gaping grin that covered his face told King that he was alright. Or at least he would be, once they were off of the island.

King watched him for a moment, glancing over his shoulder at Grace. She seemed alright and he knew that Jerry was being taken care of. Still he prayed that Jenny miraculously showed up.

"Glad to see you too." He smiled, patting Ethan on the shoulder with a grin that threatened to peel from his face. Ethan looked battered and filthy, he smelled worse. But King didn't care.

"What took you so long?" Ethan joked, returning the arm pat with gusto, nearly knocking King over. He had yet to get his land legs back after a night on the water.

"We weren't really expecting there to be an island, or a psychopath..." King was trying to stay strong so Ethan wouldn't feel like it was his fault that Jenny hadn't made it. No one had said her name since they had landed on the island. Ethan and Grace seemed too overwhelmed with relief that the search boats had made it ashore, that Colt had been found, that their ordeal was almost over.

Soon it would hit them. King glanced back at Chung, his rage radiated from him as he looked down on the man that had cost him his sister. King breathed in deeply, still holding it together. He turned back to Ethan, he was saying something.

"...bring any water with you?" He asked, looking towards the crowd of black jackets at the shore with curiosity.

"Yeah. Come on, you need to tell us where you found Colt and I've got to call that backup team in for the analysis." He put an arm on Ethan's shoulder, guiding him down the beach back to Chung and one of the captain's coolers.

He passed a bottle of water to Ethan, watching as Ethan backed away from Chung. Colt had lost consciousness again and King could feel the heat radiating off of his partner. The rage as he waited for Colt to reawaken. They all had questions for the bound man, but he was going to let Chung have this one first, it was still off the records after all. King would let him have at it until the backup arrived. He just hoped that was enough time.

Ethan gulped back the water greedily, gasping for air as he finally finished it off. King waited patiently, knowing he was worse for wear after a plane crash and a night on a strange island, not to mention a confrontation with Colt.

"He was at the cabin," Ethan began when he was finally finished the water. He could tell Chung was listening although he hadn't moved, so he spoke louder, "there's a cabin in the middle of the island. Someone probably owns this place, but Colt had it all rigged up with surveillance cameras and crazy things like at the park." He watched as Colt began to squirm, waking slowly, "Why don't you just ask him." He jabbed a thumb to the evil mastermind in the sand.

Chung smiled, reaching down to rip the gag from his mouth. Colts eyes watered, but he held his tongue, awaiting the opportune moment to spout some satirical comment to anger the agent before him. Chung picked him up by the shoulders, standing him on his bound feet. He teetered slightly before gaining his balance.

"To what do I owe this pleasure?" Colt asked dryly with a strained smile, staring euphorically into Chung's furious eyes.

For a beaten man, he held himself together quite well. He teetered in the sand at the sight of Chung's inner rage.

"What did you do to her?" Chung asked with two balled fists at his side. He wanted to know now, not after months of court dates and failed search and rescue missions. He wanted to beat it out of him, he needed to know before the rest of their team arrived. Because he knew after they did he wouldn't get a chance to speak to Colt again.

Colt looked taken back, he was quick to hide it with a Cheshire grin plastered across his face. Ethan watched their exchange with confusion.

"Who is he talking about?" He whispered to King behind Chung's back.

King turned away from the interrogation so only Ethan could see him, his face was drawn as he assessed Ethan's question. He wondered if Ethan had suffered some sort of amnesia during the plane crash. He frowned, placing a calming hand on Ethan's shoulder to break the news to him gently, unsure if it would unleash some inner turmoil that he had blocked from his head.

"Jenny," he said slowly in a quiet whisper, "she was on the plane with you, do you remember?" He held tightly to Ethan's shoulder as he watched his face contort in confusion. Suddenly Ethan turned to the trees as though he were expecting someone. King was confused, "Ethan, is Jenny..." He was afraid to ask the rest.

Ethan turned back sharply his eyes wide with realization, "Grace." He whispered, frantically. Without another word he had taken off up to the forest at a run. King glanced back to Chung, he was smacking Colt now, yelling at him for what he had done.

King shrugged, he would be alright without him. He raced after

Ethan. Wondering what he was so frantic about.

Grace was still talking with Bruce by the trees. She kept glancing to the forest watching for something eagerly. Suddenly Ethan was racing up beside her. He panted as he caught his breath, reaching for her arm frantically.

"What?" She asked, watching him suddenly worried. "What is it?" She asked again, helping him stand upright as he caught his breath.

"Jenny..." he breathed heavily, sounding like a crazed lunatic. "She's..."

"I know." Grace laughed, "No thanks to you. Bruce told me." She smiled widely, hugging Ethan as she laughed at his oversight. "It would have been nice if you had bothered to tell me in the first place, I nearly had a heart attack when the two of you came out of the woods with a body!"

King had caught up to them now, he was walking slowly as he approached, frowning at the excitement radiating off of Ethan and Grace at his mention of Jenny.

"Is there something I don't know?" He asked cautiously as the small group laughed before him.

Ethan sighed with relief, "Sorry Grace, I forgot." He pulled her in for an apologetic hug. King continued to watch in disbelief.

"About time, Ethan, you made me think my friend was dead." She slapped him lightly on the arm, "Thanks to Bruce I know better..." Bruce rolled his eyes at Ethan.

"You didn't tell her?" He laughed, "No wonder she was such a mess..."

"She's alive?" King asked hopefully, startling them as he walked closer. They all nodded in unison, "Then where is she?" He asked scanning the beach again confused.

"She's still at the cabin with Jake, they should be on their way back now. They might have taken a different path." It was Ethan who spoke now. He was embarrassed that in his haste to bring them Colt he had forgotten to tell them that Jenny was okay.

"Does Chung know?" King asked, looking down the beach to his partner. Chung was slapping Colt now, he had him on his knees in the sand and he was blue in the face from yelling. King guessed that he didn't know yet. He watched for a moment longer, sure that his partner would want to get the rage out of his system before he would let King talk to him anyway. Colt deserved it.

"Who is Jake?" King asked, now more curious than ever about the events that had transpired while he was in the water. If Grace hadn't known that Jenny was okay either, where had Jenny been? Was she really okay? Was she injured? His head was swimming with questions, but he stuck to the one.

"Jake is my best man," Bruce started, "we were on the way to my wedding, he was sitting at the back of the plane with Jenny. The plane split when it crashed." He explained, quieting as the trees began to rustle with activity, "Hello?" He called back into the brush.

"Almost there." A deep voice called from the trees.

Bruce paused in his explanation, walking closer to the trees with anticipation.

Soon two figures were emerging from the trees. Instantly there was an eruption of hugs and smiles as they were reunited with their lost companions. King was relieved to see Jenny in one piece, she seemed to be alright. Her companion on the other hand was bleeding from an arrow that still protruded from his shoulder. Soon, Bruce had whisked him away to find a medic to have it looked at, leaving Jenny alone with her friends.

"Where's the rascal?" She asked looking for her brother across the beach. King looked back to his partner across the beach with guilt as he realized that no one had told Chung the news yet. Jenny followed his eyes and spotted him, down the beach yelling at a bound Colt who was laying limp on the sand, "Ooh, he looks angry." She took off to him without another word, unaware that he thought she was dead.

SECURE

Chung had beaten Colt back into the sand. He had refused to answer a single question he had been asked, and with each moment of silence, Chung's anger grew more insatiable.

Chung's head was spinning with ideas. Colt didn't have to make it off of the island, he could easily be explained as a casualty in the crash, but he wanted his answers first and Colt knew he was safer being silent. It infuriated Chung beyond anger, he was in despair. No one had told him what had happened to Jenny. He needed to know. He wouldn't make it past today if he didn't know what had happened, his blood was boiling.

Behind him someone approached, the soft footfalls told him it wasn't King, probably more likely Grace there to comfort him. He ignored her, taking another swing at Colt and knocking him out again. She tapped him on the shoulder, he spun around stone faced.

His breath caught in his throat, his arms went slack, he blinked twice to be sure he wasn't delusional, "Jenny?" He whispered with awe.

"Well don't stop beating him on account of me," she smiled, crossing her arms, "I came down to watch." She looked expectantly over his shoulder at the limp hostage, smiling with satisfaction at the bruises and welts covering him under the sand that clung to his face.

Chung stood from his knees silently, staring at Jenny in a way that made her feel slightly uncomfortable, it verged between joy and rage, "You idiot!" He yelled, reaching out. He pulled her in for a hug, squeezing her uncomfortably tightly.

"What did I do?" She asked through his embrace, struggling to breathe over the damp coat pressed against her face.

"You made me think you were dead." His face was blank now, fighting back the emotions of joy that threatened to make his eyes well up. He held her at arm length, "Mom would have killed me." His eyes were wide with terror.

Jenny laughed now, "Gee, glad you were worried...mom would have killed me..." She mocked, pulling him back in for a real hug this time.

Behind her the others were converging on the beach. Jake walked towards them tentatively holding his freshly wrapped shoulder, the arrow still sticking awkwardly out through the white bandages. He held a hand out to Chung, "Hi, I'm Jake." He looked quizzically from Jenny to the agent, "Friend?" He asked her, hopeful.

She shook her head and his face fell, "Brother..."

"Pleasure to meet you" Jake continued shaking Chung's hand with enthusiasm, "I was stranded with your...sister... on the other side of the island. She's a great gal." He smiled to Jenny, beaming.

"Not that great..." Chung muttered under his breath, taking his hand back and glaring at his sister across the group. She had backed off at the introductions, typical Jenny. She smiled to him from behind Jake.

Before Chung had a chance to say anything more, the air was overtaken by the sound of several choppers. The rush to move out the survivors to make room for their landing had the beach alive with running and shouting over the loud windy uproar coming from overhead. Two choppers landed delicately on the beach, causing an uproar as the survivors wanting to get aboard were overtaken by the rush of armed agents escaping the doors and rushing at the beach.

With a wave of a hand they rushed in a stooped line under the still-moving propellers towards King.

"Agent King." Yelled the lead agent as he approached. "Agent Tember." He introduced himself loudly over the whir of the machines behind him. "Which way to the cabin?" He inquired. Ethan pointed to the woods where he and Bruce had emerged with Colt. Within moments half of the team had disappeared into the forest without a trace.

The agents from the second chopper were manhandling Colt back on board, replacing his cloth confines with metal cuffs as they half carried half dragged his body to the chopper. Soon they had taken off again, leaving the beach silent under the noise of their take off.

Passengers were boarded onto the first chopper as soon as the area had been cleared, moments later they were off the ground disappearing on the horizon, leaving the water rough in their wake.

Now that the island had been secured they were safe to take the rest of the stranded tourists to the boats and back to safety. King watched as the race to get to the boats became desperate, those fearful of being left behind, pushing their way to the front of the line.

King and Chung walked their group to a lone boat where their previous captain was watching the chaos in the water. He looked up as they approached, smiling with relief at the loss of aggression on Agent Chung's face.

"These ones go alone, they are in our custody." Chung said severely with a smirk, watching Jenny wade out to the boat with Jake and Bruce in tow.

"What about those two?" The captain asked, pointing at the two men with Jenny.

"Let them stay." Jenny declared defiantly helping them aboard, Chung shrugged his shoulders.

"It could be worse." He muttered to the captain with a smile.

***

The ride back to shore was relaxing, Grace watched as the island became a speck in the distance. She never wanted to see it again. She was sure the others felt the same as they stared back with her and silence washed over the boat.

One of the crew passed her a soft cotton blanket, she wrapped it around her and Ethan and let the rocking motion of the boat lull her to sleep for a moment. Finally she could relax for a moment. It took them over half an hour to reach the docks and when they arrived the commotion awoke her with a start.

News crews were swarming the area, hindering the paramedics as they tried to get the injured out of the swarm and off to the local hospital to assess their injuries. Jenny passed Jake a piece of paper before he was whisked away into an ambulance, Bruce at his side.

King and Chung, stood boldly as they waited for Jenny, Grace, Ethan and Jerry to get off of the boat. Silently they pressed forward, forming a path through the reporters as they escorted them to a black van waiting at the edge of the dock. King was relieved that they had transportation so close at hand, the reporters were savagely thrusting microphones at them as they passed. He was about ready to lose his temper by the time they reached the van, as it was he was left swatting them away so the others could climb in.

Back at the station they were held for questioning. King couldn't get them out of this one, one by one they entered a room with his senior officer and answered the questions he had about the crash. They needed probable cause to keep Colt in custody for the crash and his involvement on the island. The rest he had already been charged with formally, including charges for the chaos at the carnival. He was in for a long trial.

When it was Ethan's turn, King escorted him to the door. The room was dank and dim, he could see the men on the other side of the two way mirror. It was obvious they were not being taken too seriously as threats themselves.

He answered several questions about the flight and the letter correspondence they had received that had led them to the island via their flight to the forged safe house. Clark was a polite man, the laugh lines around his eyes crinkled when he smiled.

When he was through, he rose to shake Ethan's hand, "Thank you for your time Mr. Evans, now let's get you all to a *real* safe house."

"Thank you sir." Ethan nodded, shaking Agent Clark's hand with enthusiasm, "How will we know if my dad is safe though?" The thought had been troubling him since he had encountered Colt at the cabin. Colt knew so much about him, he had led him to his father at the carnival. Was his father safe at the hospital? How could they guarantee it after all he had just been through?

Clark looked thoughtful for a moment, as though he had considered that Ethan would ask about his father. He bowed his head as he considered what options there were for Mr. Evans Sr.. He was in critical condition at the hospital back in Monticello, they couldn't transfer him in his state without risking his life.

"I'll get a detail on him, today. Unfortunately we won't be able to move him, as I'm sure you are aware he is still quite fragile in his state." Clark nodded to Ethan, looking at the papers in his hand as he spoke. "Your safe house isn't far off, we will make sure he is taken care of." Clark was sure he had just volunteered himself for hours' worth of paperwork, he understood where Ethan was coming from, he would have expected the same if he were in that situation.

"Thank you again, Sir." Ethan beamed as he left the room to find Grace and Jerry in the waiting room. He wanted to share the news that his father would be kept safe.

Grace and Jerry were waiting for Ethan on the other side of the door, their worn faces were plastered with sorrow. He stared at Grace for a moment, reaching for her hand as he worried about her sudden sadness. They were finally safe, what could be wrong now?

"Ethan." King approached from behind Grace, placing a hand on Ethan's shoulder, "You should sit down for a moment." He pulled Ethan forward to a row of chairs, allowing Grace and Jerry to collapse into the chairs beside him.

Ethan's world was spinning. He looked across the room for Jenny and Chung, wondering if one of them had sustained serious injuries that would cause such a panic. They were both sitting silently across the room looking at him with regret. He had no idea what was going on.

"King?" He asked, "What's going on? Aren't we safe now?"

King stared at him for a moment, Clark came rushing out of the room behind them, "King." He whispered, phone in hand as he assessed the room and went silent. Gaping at the scene before him.

"Ethan," King began, knowing it was now or never, "Your father, he didn't make it."

He waited for a minute while Ethan process the information, beside him Grace began to weep again. She had held herself together long enough for King to break the news, but hearing it again tore a fresh hole in her heart and she couldn't keep it in any longer. Ethan pulled her in close, resting his chin on her head as his blank face began to lose color.

"How?" Was all he could say.

***

Ethan was silent during the drive to the safe house. He hadn't quite had time to wrap his head around what was going on. It felt like he was sitting in a fog, he was aware that others were around him, Grace's hand grasped firmly in his. Yet he couldn't really see them there, he couldn't focus on anything but the scene in his mind.

Colt had gotten his last shot in after all. He had stopped at the hospital before the flight and passed himself off as a nurse working on Mr. Evans' floor. It had been too late before they realized he had been overdosed. He hadn't stood a chance.

Ethan breathed in heavily, wondering how he was going to put himself back together after this. He still had Grace and Jerry, his mind rationalized. But he would never have another chance to get his father back.

It seemed so final this time. It had seemed final the first time and that made it even harder for him now, there was a nagging voice in the back of his mind telling him that he could save his father like he already had. Something inside of him honestly through that if he looked hard enough he would find him alive again. He couldn't help but indulge that thought to ease the pain of the truth. This was it.

The drive was a long one, but the agents suspected that the passengers they were transferring had no interest in getting onto another plane for a long while. Most of them slept in the back while King drove. He could tell that Ethan was still awake, silently staring through the back window into the darkness. He knew Ethan was taking the news of his father quite badly. He was still lost in the shock of the plane crash, he hadn't wanted to burden his friend with more bad news. It would take Ethan a while to work his way around to believing that his father was really and truly gone, King understood that. He drove faster, wanting to get the drive over with so Ethan could finally rest.

King was taking them back to Monticello, not to their house but to a safe location close by. He and Chung had been permitted to stay with them for the remainder of their stay, mostly because of Jenny. Chung had refused outright to trust another agent with his sister's wellbeing. Agent Clark had taken his request seriously and assigned two other agents to work with them to provide around the clock security to the four until Colt was brought to trial. It would be a bit of a vacation for him after the trials they had all endured. He wasn't sure he was looking forward to the quiet life. Behind him the cavalcade of caravans kept pace with his lead foot as he sped down the highway into the night.

FINIS

Ethan sat silently as the wall of black suits surrounded him. Grace was by his side, Jenny and Jerry in front as they exited the black caravan. They had been in exile for a week now, Ethan had barely spoken a word.

Grace leaned on him as they walked, her black dress whispering in the light breeze. She was crying already, Jerry and Jenny had fallen into step beside her, holding one another tight for support. The barrage of body guards blocking their view of the cemetery.

The ceremony was a short one, Ethan was still in denial as he watched his father's casket lowering into the ground at his feet. Grace clung to his arm with a firm grip, holding him from peering too far in.

King stood beside him, hands clasped at his belt, head nodded to his chest.

They had been permitted to leave the sanctuary of their safe house for Ethan's father's funeral. As Ethan glanced up at the gathering around him he realized just how much work had gone into this one trip. He was grateful that they had made an allowance for him. He could see beyond King, the fleet of special ops monitoring the perimeter of the churchyard with vigilance. How had his life become so complicated?

Soon they were walking back to the waiting van, the moment had passed in a daze for Ethan. He was sure he would recount it again tonight as he failed to sleep and his mind raced off on him.

Agent Clark waited for them at the van. As Ethan approached, he stopped.

"Ethan," he began sheepishly, "I am so sorry for your loss." He bowed his head apologetically, wondering if Ethan blamed him for his father's death. He should have put a security detail on Mr. Evans as soon as he had entered the hospital, he wished he hadn't had the oversight. His thin smile extended farther as he pulled out an envelope from his brief case, "I wanted to deliver this to you in person. Congratulations." He passed the envelope over to Ethan before walking away with one backward glance. Ethan stared at it with anticipation the emblem on the back was raised and sent a shiver down his spine. He peeled back the envelope revealing the pages inside.

It was a letter from the Academy. He had sent in an application months ago and completely forgotten about it. He had been accepted to join the Federal Bureau's training academy, his heart leapt in his chest. King was still waiting for him by the door to escort him back to the safe house. Ethan passed him the sheet with a quiet smile.

King looked it over with a large smile plastered across his face, "It's about time."

Ethan knew he would make his father proud.

ABOUT THE AUTHOR

Katlin Murray lives in Ontario with her family. She enjoys reading to her children and watching old movies with her husband.

Made in the USA
Middletown, DE
14 October 2021